TAINTED HARVEST

SIMONE DOUCET SERIES BOOK 1

E. DENISE BILLUPS

"They came at night... a horde of starving vagabonds, homeless, helpless, and pitiable..."

— W.E.B. DU BOIS

FOR THOSE WHOSE STORY WAS NEVER TOLD.

UNKNOWN STANZA

PRESENT-DAY BROOKLYN, NEW YORK

"WELCOME HOME, MONI."

"Home . . ." The taxi swerves around a sharp corner, tossing Simone across the back seat into the door, jarring her from sleep. Lost to her whereabouts for a moment, she lifts her gaze up the divider and across the confined space, to the in-cab TV, certain she'd heard her mother's voice. She raises herself off the leather seat, unfurls her stiff body and jet-lagged mind, recalling the late-night dinner party, racing to catch a flight to the States, and stumbling into the taxi half asleep at JFK Airport.

The driver eyes her in the rearview mirror.

Was it his voice she heard? "Did you say something a moment ago?"

"No, Miss." His brows furrow at her confusion. "Long trip?"

She nods, "Yes. France." Rubbing her eyes, she glances out the rain-mottled taxi window at the approaching four-story brownstone. Home again, but there's no one to welcome her back from her trip. Dark windows reflect the gray day and vacant interior as the cab comes to a stop. Comfort, which she often feels when returning from an assignment, recedes with the

1

deluge that pummeled the taxi from the airport straight to her apartment stoop.

She steps into a curbside puddle with a silent expletive, splashing toward the turban-headed cabbie as he removes her luggage from the trunk to the sidewalk, pressing and jerking on the stubborn handle several times.

"Please, let me get that."

"No, Miss, I got it," he replies with a stronger tug. "There we go," he says with a victorious grin as though he'd accomplished an intricate feat, placing the handle in her outstretched hand.

"Thank you," she says, handing him a generous tip, which garners a gracious smile and a palm-to-chin bow from the Indian man.

"Namaste. Welcome home, Miss."

"Thank you." Though his welcome isn't the intimate reception home she yearns for, it engenders a sincere smile.

"Taxi! Wait!"

"Another fare," she says to the cabbie, pointing over his shoulder at the couple running toward the taxi.

He pivots his head toward the intersection, then back at her, pausing with an odd glare that causes Simone to frown and wipe her cheeks, afraid there's something other than rain on her face.

His lips purse then narrow. "Rain brings good harvests and much enlightenment," he says with a nod of affirmation as if telling her fortune. "And it brings many passengers." He smiles with a final bow, turns, and signals with a hand wave to the couple, angling his body into the driver's seat.

Was that a customary Indian farewell? Too jet-lagged to consider his strange expression and words, she turns and glances up, catching movement in her bedroom window on the upper floor. When nothing appears, she wonders if it was just birds flitting on a tree limb.

She looks away and pulls her luggage up ten steps and stops at the stained-glass double doors of the Brooklyn Heights brownstone she's shared two years with three wayfaring roommates who travel for work as often as she does. The four-story flat, dubbed "the layover," serves as a respite from their hectic lifestyles. For a week or two at most, their paths crisscross and the brownstone assumes a dormitory vibe—alive with music, chatter, and dinner parties—until work calls them elsewhere again.

"Layover" is a perfect description, given her roomies, Jude, Mitchell, and Stacy, could move to another city for work at any time. And the landlord, Eric Lawson, might not renew the lease next year. The Lawson family has owned the brownstone since the roaring twenties when their ancestors migrated to the city with countless other immigrants during the Jazz Age. Eric, who lives in a larger home on Long Island, prefers renting the sandstone relic to selling it. He pops in once a month to check his property, always catching her off guard. She suspects he visits when they're away but hopes he doesn't snoop through their belongings.

Simone pulls the graphite-gray Samsonite luggage over the threshold and steps onto the "Welcome" doormat. Heeding the "NO SHOES ALLOWED" plaque, she slips off her sodden wellies, protecting magnificent bamboo floors from sidewalk germs and grime. She hangs her Burberry trench on the foyer rack and wipes rain from her brow, alert to the silence of the first floor as well as the upper floors.

Remembering the shadow she'd seen from the stoop in the window, she calls, "Hello! Anyone home?" Her voice reverberates around the walls, disturbing the silent home with no response.

"Alone again," she mumbles, placing the key on the foyer table and detaching her laptop bag from the Samsonite.

A fusty odor from the humid weather seeps from the upholstery in the living room, reeking of a seldom-visited cabin in a moss-laden forest. Moving toward the large sectional, she glares at the tranquil space, places the laptop on the coffee table, and saunters across the room, lifting the shades of three rain-flecked floor-to-ceiling bay windows to find a dreary picture of the tree-lined promenade and thick clouds mushrooming over New York Harbor and lower Manhattan's skyline. A three-million-dollar view worthy of the steep rent.

Letters and magazines fill Jude's, Stacy's, and her own mail slot in the rotating carousel on the sideboard created to organize their mail. Mitchell's empty compartment confirms that he was there last. Among a plethora of bills and junk mail, she recognizes a pink envelope with the HBM logo, suspecting it contains payment for last month's assignment on fine dining in New Orleans, a piece she enjoyed writing, as she'd visited the city many times for Mardi Gras and knew most of the regular haunts and restaurants in town.

She slits the envelope flap open with her fingernail, finding a check creased between gold-embossed, ivory HBM stationery edged in colorful, swirling flower bouquets—a letter from *Happy Brides Magazine*'s editor. Placing the banknote on the table, she drifts to the sofa and reads.

Simone,

Your New Orleans article last month was impressive. The team and I believe you're the perfect person to cover our upcoming July Southern Peach Edition. We need a Travel Writer to highlight a well-known Victorian Bed-and-Breakfast on the bluffs of Natchez, Mississippi, overlooking the River. Natchez boasts historical tourist attractions, antebellum mansions that serve as hotels, and Victorian B&Bs for a fabu-

*lous southern honeymoon getaway. I've heard the city
has many peach orchards. It would be lovely to give
our readers a taste of Mississippi. A wonderful peach
dessert or drink at your discretion. If you're interested
in the assignment, please let me know soon so we can
make travel arrangements.*

*Amelia and Parker Randolph, the owners of the B&B,
and old college mates, graciously offered free accom-
modations for your visit. As natives of the state, they
possess a wealth of knowledge of the city's history,
tourist attractions, or any information you need for
the article. They're a wonderful couple, and I guar-
antee you'll have a fabulous time.*

*Simone, I know you will do a fantastic job. I look for-
ward to reading your article.*

Happy Travel Writing!
Bridgette Witcombe, Editor
Happy Bride Magazine (HBM)

"Another assignment? Geez, give me a chance to
breathe," she grumbles, surprised Bridgette's granted
more work before the submission of her current article.
Three assignments in less than a month and having just
returned from a trip to France, she can't imagine hop-
ping on another plane so soon. She stares around the
quiet room and sighs, realizing she'll soon feel captive
within these walls and yearn for another escape, as always. Removing the laptop from its gray-turquoise case
with a world map pattern, she opens the incomplete article on France. A final revision and she'll remit to Bridgette the next day.

Jet-lagged and yearning for something more comfortable than her rumpled travel clothes, Simone grabs
her suitcase in the foyer, heads to her bedroom, un-

dresses, and slips into her robe. She inspects her room, a smaller version of the living room, with octagonal walls and three floor-to-ceiling bay windows, smelling of sandalwood and lavender, remnants of candles, laundered sheets, and lavender sachets placed in the closet. Captivated by Moroccan décor on assignment in Morocco two years before, she purchased Moroccan pillows and rugs to center the arching window seat. Four tall rustic Moroccan lantern holders sit inside the firebox and two on opposite ends of the decorative hearth, giving the nonworking fireplace a fiery ambiance whenever she's home. Over the mantel, in soothing turquoise ocean blue, hangs a lengthy Moroccan tapestry.

She catches her reflection in the wall mirror and combs her fingers through the new pixie cut, a rash decision made in France. Tired of fussing with unmanageable curls, she walked into Les Cocottes salon on rue de l'évêché in Marseille.

The hairdresser with creamy milk-chocolate skin and thick auburn box braids stared in shock at her request, trying to change her mind. *"Non, ce n'est pas vrai. Ces cheveux merveilleux. Je peux le style pour toi, non?"* No, such wonderful hair. I can style for you, no?

Simone sat in the chic, pink-and-black hydraulic chair and demanded, *"Coupez-le."* Chop it off.

The hairdresser sighed. *"Comme vous le souhaitez."* As you wish.

Simone closed her eyes and listened to the Japanese shear's snip, snip, feeling her shoulder-length strands fall around her, wondering if she'd regret it later. When she heard the hairdresser's *"Ooh, aww . . . Magnifique,"* she opened her eyes to the three-way mirror. Lily, her mother, stared back. She looked like a younger version of her mom, who'd worn her hair short most of her life. She studied her heart-shaped face, cinnamon-brown eyes, and the sandy brown pixie cut, knowing she'd made the right decision.

She strolled carefree and liberated through Marseille's uneven streets, admiring the shape of her head and long elegant neck in shop windows along the Rue Saint Ferreol. Unfettered by windblown hair, she wandered along pebble beaches in Anse de Maldormé and snapped photos of medieval hilltop villages and crumbling 10th-century castles at Château des Baux. Hair fanned above her scalp like grass in mistral winds. It was the boldest decision she'd ever made without regret.

She ties the robe sash around her waist, heads downstairs, and frowns through the living room's variegated windowpanes at another downpour. The soggy weather affects a need for a hot cup of tea to dispel the damp chill. She drags her sluggish body into the kitchen, feet scuffing against the wooden floor. Too tired to run water in the kettle or wait for it to boil, she microwaves a cup and steeps a blueberry chamomile tea bag in the steaming water.

A weary sigh deflates her chest as her sluggish legs carry her drifting back to the sofa. She stares at the unfinished article on the laptop, recalling the luxurious suite she'd stayed in for two weeks. A life she could never afford on a travel writer's salary. But money hasn't been an issue since her mother, Lily, passed away four months ago. When her father disclosed the thirty-year-old policy from her employer and two personal insurances she'd purchased several months before her death, disbelief ensued.

Little had her mother known that six months later an unknown heart condition would claim her in sleep. Or maybe she had an inkling her time was short and that was the reason she bought additional insurance. Simone's heart sinks, recalling her father's distressed phoned call the day Lily died and how he had grasped for words, barely forming sentences.

"Simone . . . Lily . . ." he'd said with an anguished pause.

"Dad? You there?"

"She didn't . . ."

"What's wrong? Is Mom OK?"

"She didn't wake up this morning."

"Is she sick?"

"No, she couldn't wake up."

"She's probably working too hard and needs to rest a few extra hours. She needs this trip to France. I've booked the flight and hotel. All she needs to do is be ready to go. She'll get plenty of rest and enjoy herself—"

"No, hon . . ." His voice tremored and cracked. He placed his hand over the receiver to muffle tears as he gathered his composure. *"Lily's gone . . . She passed in her sleep. The doctor said it was a heart attack."*

His words snatched her breath from her chest and her legs out from under her. If a chair hadn't been nearby, she would have collapsed in a heap on the floor. Remarkably enough, through her shock, she'd found the wherewithal to question what was an improbable heart attack.

"No, no, Dad, that's impossible!" she'd screamed, bursting into a tearful tirade. *"Mom gets an annual checkup every year, and there were no signs of heart trouble and no genetic predisposition. She's the healthiest woman I know. Never touched process food or alcohol. Walked several miles a day. She can't just go to sleep and never wake up!"*

Simone lamented a long time, recalling the words her Mom had spoken just days before she passed. "I'm so fortunate," she had said, "to have a wonderful job and adoring family." She was enthusiastic about her work as a Research Librarian at Louisiana State University, never stressed, and comforted by aisles of books. After all the years of hard work, she deserved that trip to France.

Simone couldn't imagine going without her until her grief-stricken father took her place. Traveling with her cremains, they scattered a small amount in the River

Seine, a place Mom had dreamt of visiting for years. They had been unsure where the last of her ashes should rest, so they had chosen to keep them above the mantel until a place was determined.

For months, Simone was in disbelief and questioned Lily's heart attack. Nagging instincts wouldn't let it be. And even now, she believes something else caused her death. But why did she buy two additional insurance policies? Did she know about the heart condition? And if she had, why keep it a secret? Did prescience or sensibilities spur her decision to buy more financial security for the family?

It appears she prepared for the inevitable, leaving her university pension and insurance policies to secure their future. Mom worried travel writing might not earn her only child a decent living, but so far, she's been lucky to have consistent work. She'd relinquish every cent of the wretched insurance proceeds earning dividends and interest in her investment account to see her mom alive again.

Losing his wife and having only one child, her widowed father worries and incessantly reminds her, "A single woman traveling alone isn't safe." Evils of the world always keep her hypervigilant, never straying far from crowds, and emailing her itinerary to her father and friends. Fear hasn't stopped her from enjoying work.

She figures at twenty-six, there's plenty of time to travel before settling on a more stable career. After college, she submitted a writing sample to the well-established online magazine *Happy Brides*, not expecting a response. To her surprise, a month later and just as she'd lost faith and was considering a more stable desk job with a nonprofit organization, the editor called. For four years, Bridgette, the founder and editor of the magazine, has been a godsend and a good friend, always finding assignments when Simone needs the work.

For a trial period during the first year, Bridgette assigned domestic trips as preparation for something bigger. After fourteen months of traveling up and down the East and West Coasts, she got the chance to travel to the Caribbean and foreign destinations she'd always dreamt of visiting. The stamps in her passport and collections of postcards and photos paint a picture of a life of nonstop exotic travels to Barcelona, Cairo, Dublin, Maldives, Morocco, Paris, Scottish Highlands, Seychelles, and more. The Samsonite suitcase functions as a permanent closet. Hotels as temporary homes. And strangers along the way become new friends, welcoming her back from a nomadic life.

She loves her hometown, Baton Rouge, Louisiana, but could never spend her entire life in one place as her parents have. They always said, "No one will embrace you like your own people." Isn't that true of every culture? She's never let other's narrow-mindedness hinder her life. She wondered if fear prevented her parents from traveling to other countries, as they never ventured far from Louisiana. Her mother had welcomed and loved postcards from various destinations and eagerly awaited every one of her articles. She wished they'd had the opportunity to travel together before Lily's death. They certainly could have, but something kept them rooted.

Unlike her parents, she longs for diversity, and perhaps this is the reason she enjoys traveling the world and making a home in Brooklyn's multicultural community. She believes her travels are ventures toward something meaningful but always returns with the same sense of emptiness, hoping the next trip will fill the void. Maybe her friends are right—travel writing is pure escapism, avoidance of significant work. Writing about something more profound than honeymoon destinations might inspire greater satisfaction.

Faint scents of Marseille's Mediterranean mistral's

garrigue that clung to her clothes and skin, wafts from her body as she collapses back into the sofa. Spice and pine mixed with stale cigarette fumes she hadn't had time to wash off after the previous evening's rooftop dinner after oversleeping and having to rush to catch a flight to the States the next morning. She'd shared a rich cassoulet and abundant glasses of malbec wine with Anya's family, friends she'd made a year ago on her first assignment in Marseille. The classic meal reminded her of her mother's spicy gumbo. No one, not even she, makes gumbo so savory, tendered with the perfect roux, thick with crawfish, andouille sausage, stewed tomatoes, and okra.

A loud patter against the window pulls her gaze toward the worsening downpour. Sinking further into the sofa, she lifts the teacup to her nose, inhales rising blueberry aroma, closes her eyes, and ponders the new assignment. Why does the city of Natchez sound familiar? Maybe she'd heard it from her family, who often spoke of friends in Mississippi. She takes a sip of tea and places the mug on the table.

"Natchez . . . Natchez," she repeats, tapping the envelope on her bottom lip. Conceivably, she'd seen the city name on a freeway destination sign when she traveled to a classmate's wedding in Jackson, Mississippi, three summers ago during the worst heatwave she ever recalls and cares never to experience again.

Simone yawns aloud, her eyes sinking further into her sockets. The time zone and late-night party take a toll finally. Unable to lift her heavy eyelids, she allows the intense urge to sleep fall over her weary body and mind.

~

Minutes later, an odorous dampness and movement stir her awake. She lifts her head from the sofa, lost to her whereabouts for an instant, pondering how long she'd slept, and glances toward the foyer.

"Stacy? Jude? Mitchell? Anyone home?" she calls, believing someone entered the brownstone, waking her from sleep. No. They would have answered her or come into the living room in their usually noisy arrival.

She sits straight, alarmed by the quiet. If possible, the silent room quietens further, as though smothered by another layer of air. Only once had Simone experienced this sensation—on a coal-black night in Baton Rouge when a passing hurricane deadened electricity in the home. But the lights are on in the brownstone.

Simone turns her head right and sniffs.

What is that?

Smells like fruit . . . Mangoes? Plums? No, peaches. Not again . . . The last time she returned home from a trip, a sickening musk saturated the space from assorted fruits rotting in a syrupy soup on the dining table.

When an evanescent flicker moves in her periphery, she twists her head, catching a fruity scent emanating from the sectional's corner. A chill ripples down her arm, not from cold, for the room is warm, but from an uncanny sensation, alerting her senses. Pale light from the window flickers across the floor, bouncing onto the rolled sofa arm. She releases a sigh. It must be a passing car or light from the promenade.

She lowers her head into the plush pillows and sniffs to the edge of the sofa, believing humid weather has drawn embedded odors from the upholstery. The synthetic smell of microfiber and age-old musk fills her nostrils.

The kitchen.

Rising from the sofa, she drifts past the dining area into the L-shaped galley, finding ripe but unspoiled Granny Smith apples on the counter. Back in the living room, she glances around before taking a seat on the sofa, wondering if she'd imagined the smell. A mere second after she sits, the scent returns. An obscure lyric invades her thoughts as though someone whispered in her ear.

Below the bluffs of Natchez Trace, the Devil's Eden lies in waste.

The cryptic words prickle her spine. A presence beside her stirs the air. An alarming tightness constricts her chest as she anxiously turns her head and stares into space, searching for the inscrutable essence. She lowers her hand onto the cool cushion with a head shake, laughing at her foolishness.

What are you doing?

Nothing's there. Positing the scent and whisper were just figments of a jet-lagged mind, she retrieves the HBM envelope that slipped to the floor when she dozed off. The Natchez assignment and mention of peaches triggered the fruity redolence and some long-forgotten poem or song. Is it a refrain she'd heard in Louisiana as a child? But the adventitious lyric didn't sound familiar.

She stares hard at the laptop, lifts it onto her thighs, and logs into her email, debating whether to call or email Bridgette. Too exhausted to compose an email or fetch her cell phone in the foyer, she FaceTimes Bridgette from the laptop.

The phone rings five times. Just as she's about to hang up, an invisible person picks up and a distant muffled voice somewhere in the room says, "Hold on." On the screen, a bright white backdrop decorated with gold-framed family photos and abstract paintings emerge beside a window overlooking Manhattan's West End Avenue.

Bridgette's head rises with disheveled blonde strands covering her face at the bottom of the screen. She places something on the desk with a thud, pushes hair off her face, sitting back in the chair with a breathy exhalation. "Oh, hi, love. Sorry, I spilled my drink under the desk trying to get to the laptop. Ah! Simone! Look at you. Your hair looks gorgeous. If I didn't know it was you, I'd think Halle Berry FaceTimed me accidentally," she says with a chortle. "You look like a younger version of her."

"Not Rihanna? How about Josephine Baker," Simone suggests waggishly, twisting her head left to right and up and down, showcasing the cut.

Bridgette scrunches her face in consideration. A pink flush colors her pale cheeks. "Um . . . Nah, definitely Halle," Bridgette says, shaking her head. "When did you arrive home, love?"

"Only moments ago."

"Did you receive my letter and payment for the New Orleans article?"

"It arrived before Marseille's scent wore off my skin," she quips. "But I'm not complaining. I can always use the money and another opportunity to travel. So, without further ado, I'm thrilled to accept the Natchez assignment."

"Oh, love, that's great!" she says with a slight British lilt that's faded since she moved with the love of her life to the States several years ago.

"I've heard of Natchez but never been to the city. I'm looking forward to a new town and meeting Parker, and Amelia. And I know the perfect dessert our readers will crave. Peach cobbler. It was my mother's specialty and favorite dessert."

"Très southern."

Très . . . Simone chuckles at Bridgette's new word. Last month it was fabulous, the month before brilliant, words abandoned like last year's fashion trends. What catchphrase will augment her lexicon in July? She smirks inwardly. "Yes, très southern," she mimics and smiles. "Natchez is not too far from my parent's home in Baton Rouge, so it gives me a chance to visit my dad after the assignment. Bridge, what do you know about Natchez?"

"Only what I've heard from Parker and Amelia and read on the state's website. Why do you ask?"

"Before I called you, the strangest lyric about Natchez popped into my head."

"An anthem, like New York's big apple song?"

"God, I hope not. It's rather cryptic."

"Let's hear it."

"Below the bluffs of Natchez Trace, the Devil's Eden lies in waste."

"Yipes! That's downright creepy. Gave me goosebumps," Bridgette says, brushing her arm. "Nope, haven't heard it and would never forget those words. You should ask Parker and Amelia when you get to the city. I'm sure they will know."

"Of course, it's their hometown. Oh, when does the assignment start?"

"Look, here's the thing. The B&B's booked all summer, so Parker only has a room available next week, of course at no cost to us. They can book you in the Bluffside suite with a private patio and gorgeous views of the Mississippi River on Monday for seven days."

"Next Monday?"

"Vrooooooooooom!"

Bridgette's five-year-old son's blonde head pops sideways on the screen. He circles her chair with a toy plane above her head, making zooming sounds. Annoyed, she snatches the plane, places it on the desk, and pulls him into her arms. "I'm talking to Simone. Don't be rude, OK?"

Brett nods his head. Bridgette ruffles his floppy mane and looks back at the screen. "Sorry, Brett gets restless this time of night."

"No worries." Simone perceives the frustration she's caught on Bridgette's face many times, though Bridgette has grown more patient with motherhood in the last year.

"Love, if you need more time, Amelia and Parker

can offer a smaller room adjoined to their suite, but you'd have to share their bath."

"Certainly not! I don't want to impose on their privacy. I'll take the Bluff-side suite Monday. Four days at home is more than enough time to recuperate from France." Simone yawns, covering her mouth.

"You look exhausted, but I hope the trip was worth it?"

"Amazing, amazing, amazing! Every moment was superb. You'll see when I email the article, but it needs one final tweak and I'll send it tomorrow." Another yawn skews her face. "Ooh! Excuse me," she squeals midst a wider yawn.

Bridgette chuckles. "Someone besides my son needs to be in bed."

Brett frowns and hides his sleepy face in her shoulder.

"Hey, don't worry about sending the article tomorrow. It's not due for two days. You need to recuperate for your next trip. Now go and get some z's, love."

"Thanks, Bridgette. I will as soon as we hang up."

"Oh, by the way, love, love, love the hair. It's très chic and suits you well. Brett, say goodbye to Simone."

"Bye-bye," he mutters, snatching the toy plane, varooming it through Bridgette's hair and racing from her arm.

"Ahh, you little brat," she screams at his vanishing figure.

Simone chuckles. "He's adorable."

Bridgette huffs, fixing her hair with a scowl. "He's a little rascal. Gotta put him to bed before he gets into more trouble. Bye-bye for now. Sleep well, sweetheart," Bridgette says, blowing a kiss through the screen.

Simone blows a kiss back, ending the call. Too jetlagged to cook or edit the article, she laces her fingers around the teacup, inhales the blueberry-scented steam, and reclines between two oversized decorative pillows.

She lifts her head, fixing her gaze past the window on Manhattan's skyline illuminated in brooding skies. Before fatigue overtakes her, she opens the Internet browser and types "Natchez, Mississippi."

The city's official website explodes with images of antebellum mansions with tall white pillars, oaks dripping with Spanish moss, and tulip magnolia trees; a quaint downtown with antique dealers and coffee shops, restaurants and cafes, and horse-and-buggy tours; casino riverboats on the Mississippi River streaming past forested bluffs; ancient cemeteries with angel effigies that appear to move; and, like most southern towns, a haunted ghost tour.

Another picture-perfect site, hiding Natchez's impoverished neighborhoods. Why is Bridgette interested in Natchez? It's no different from any other southern town, and it can't be just their peaches. What's the focal point of her article? It must be her friend's bed-and-breakfast, but if not, she needs to uncover something unique to Natchez before she makes the trip.

She yawns and continues browsing the Internet, pondering Bridgette's interest in Natchez peaches. Isn't Georgia the peach capital? If her memory's correct, Mississippi's known for its abundance of blueberries. She types Natchez peach orchards in the search bar, surprised to find only links to apple and blueberry orchards. "Hmpf . . ."

When a WhatsApp text message slides across the top of the Mac, she glances at her wristwatch, still on France's time, 2:15 a.m., and at the time on the laptop, 8:15 p.m., New York time. Why's Anya up so late? Opening the message, she yawns wider and reads.

> *Simone, I hope you've made it home safely. Give me a call tomorrow when you're settled in.*
>
> *Anya*

xoxo

Simone responds immediately.

Anya, you're up late. I'm back in rainy Brooklyn and missing everyone and sunny France. I will call you tomorrow after I've caught up on sleep. Thanks for allowing me to stay at your fabulous home and spend time with your delightful family the last days of my trip. It was the best part of my visit. Speak soon.

Simone
xoxo

Anya's concern warms her heart, comforted someone cares she made it home safe. Her mom always checked on her after a trip and always kept her travel itinerary. So does her father, who called her just as she entered the taxi at JFK International Airport. She checks her email, text messages, and voicemail, finding a welcome home text from Roderick Doucet, her father, and a two-week-old email from her roommate Mitchell she's avoided opening since their last night together before leaving for France.

She'd ignored the attraction between them for as long as she could. During a moment of weakness, they had both succumbed to a moment of need, an inebriated kiss. A mistake she regrets. When she mentioned it to Bridgette, she'd said, "Don't shit where you eat." She's direct, but always right. A relationship with Mitchell is not what she needs. He's a male version of her, noncommittal and always searching for something greater than love. Besides, she can't afford to screw up her roomies' perfect living arrangement.

DREAMS

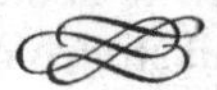

Contemplating the climb to the second floor, she closes and lifts the laptop, forcing herself off the comfortable sectional before fatigue cements her to the sofa for the night. She shuffles upstairs, listening to silent upper floors, her movement the only sound in the home. At moments like this, she misses her roomies, dreading sleeping alone in such a colossal place. Past three quiet rooms to the end of the narrow hall, she enters her bedroom, locking the door behind her.

She places the laptop on the dual-purpose pedestal table, used as a nightstand and a desk, beside the midnight-cherry wood sleigh bed centering the room. Both pieces left behind, as was most of the home's furniture when the Lawson family moved. She prefers the sparse, ready-to-go-at-a-moment's-notice aesthetic.

Slipping from her robe into an oversized T-shirt, she proceeds toward the mantel, lighting each candle around the hearth and gazing at the mosaic of shadows cast by the lantern's metal lattice pattern. The cryptic lyric repeats like a broken record in her head, struggling for the next word. "Below the bluffs of Natchez Trace, the Devil's Eden lies in waste . . ." she recites again, reclining on the edge of the bed.

She retrieves the laptop from the table and types "songs and poems on Natchez" in the browser, receiving unrelated search results. When she types the lyric's exact words, the search engine populates the page with a Christian website, biblical verses on the Garden of Eden, and a site about Natchez Trace, a historic 440-mile forest trail stretching from Nashville, Tennessee, to Natchez, Mississippi.

After several minutes, her head dips and rolls upright as she struggles to stay awake. Her eyes open to a webpage displaying a forested cliff. The view spirals down through a thicket of trees to the banks of the Mississippi. The image swivels as if someone's turning in circles with a camera. Simone's eyes widen when a ghastly face flickers across the screen and vanishes. The website darkens, returning to the home page.

"What was that?"

She back clicks, unable to find the site. When she types the stanza into the browser again, the strange website doesn't materialize. Drunk with weariness, she places the laptop back on the table, failing to see the screen flash and fade on a forested area near the banks of the Mississippi River.

Beneath lavender-scented sheets, her gaze drifts to the Okame Cherry tree flanking the casement, peak pink when she left for France, now a deep green. Raindrops tap against the window, fading to white noise as images of Marseille and castle ruins flit in nonsensical patterns in her mind. Deep in sleep, a fruity aroma seeps into her dream.

Clanging metal wakes Simone to an unfamiliar room. Floral bouquets and roses circle the space. Through an open patio door, a sweet aroma wafts in moonlight, bathing the humid night. A scraggy girl in tattered clothes flows on mud-caked feet toward the entrance. Chains braid her swollen belly, trailing her soiled petticoat hem, clanging over garden stones. She cradles a cloaked bounty, wafting pungent into the room, curling mesmeric around Simone. Her glassy pupils drop to her round belly, flattening as a bundle rumbles from beneath her skirt onto timber floors. Moonlight elongates her quivering shadow across a carpet of grass as she turns, drifting past the door.

Entranced, Simone slides to the edge of the high bed and descends a three-rung bed step, drifting toward tall glass French doors. A ruby-gold trail rolls from beneath the girl's ragged skirt, a reptilian appendage to her bony tail, slithering beyond a row of shrubs. Simone bends and scoops a plump peach bowling from the bush to her feet, running her nose along the corpulent downy skin with a deep inhalation. A voice rises from the shrubbery.

"Sweeeeeeeet . . . Bite it!"

Her hypnotic tone goads an uncontrollable, mouthwatering bite into the intoxicating flesh. Bittersweet pulp spurts her brow, soaks her lips, dribbles chin to breast, streaming from hand to wrist.

With closed eyes, she delights in every bite, craving more, scraping the rough core. Juice curdles her gut with each ravenous taste of the pulsating mass. Her teeth loosen on the skeletal pit, falling rotten from her mouth, oozing crimson seeds to her wrist. Retching with abdominal pain, she spits pulp from her mouth, tosses the peach, and clutches her growing, bloated belly as something wriggles and kicks inside. Somber hymns rise in masses behind the shrubbery with her groaning agony.

The girl's gray phalanges worm through boughs, snatching and puncturing her wrist with poisonous fingernails. A crimson rash rises on her flesh, pulsing with pus, branching up her arm to scabs, hardening to woody shoots sprouting pink blossoms.

Whites of the girl's coal-black eyes flood viscous tar, sockets glistening genesis of imageries.

Afraid to see, Simone squeezes her eyes shut.

"Open yo eyes. See my horror!" the girl demands as wretched voices rise, a piercing hymn in the dark.

"Below the bluffs of Natchez Trace,
The Devil's Eden lies in waste.
A tainted harvest sinfully laced,
Corse sowed and reaped,
Reptilian chawed,
Rotted silt loam,
A charnel house,
Below the bluffs of Natchez Trace . . ."

Simone thrashes, rolling around the bed, moaning and squirming, springing upright with a scream. A shadow spirals from the ceiling then recedes into the candlelight's lattice patterns. She twists her head around, searching the octagonal room for the wraith-like girl. Glancing at her arm and pushing her tongue against her teeth, she exhales in relief. Tartness coats her tongue, and her palm vibrates from the throbbing peach.

"Impossible. How could I feel and taste in a dream?"

She wipes her lips, brushes her tongue across her teeth, and swallows tart figments away. A spasm bites and grips her abdomen with moisture saturating her panties. She moans, presses her palm to her stomach, and whips the sheet from her body to find a blood-splotched sheet. "No, can't be," she mutters. Her monthly just ended two weeks ago and isn't due until the end of June.

She rushes to the bathroom, examining her flesh-colored bikini briefs, spotted dark red, realizing the excruciating pain in her dream was cramping.

The bitter taste in her mouth nauseates. She opens her mouth, searching her teeth and tongue, then stops and laughs at her foolishness.

"It was just a dream," she utters, spreading toothpaste on the brush, scrubbing her teeth and tongue, rinsing several times until clean peppermint suppresses the bitter aftertaste.

Loose rotting teeth.

The dream interpretation means death.

Ridiculous . . .

The images were just an assemblage in her unconscious mind of the Natchez assignment, the strange lyric, and Internet research, she thinks.

Scuzzy from travel grime, the clammy dream, and her monthly, she slips off her T-shirt and panties and hurries into the shower, washing remnants of Marseille, bloody peach figments, and her menses away.

Moments later, showered, lying on clean bedsheets, and staring at the ceiling, vivid images of the girl, the unfamiliar room, and the patio resurface. The grass felt real beneath her feet, the pulsing peach, a heart in her hand, the pit appeared human bones. The solemn hymn plays in her mind. She repeats the words several times, pulls the laptop from the table, and types the stanza up to the last line—"Rotted silt loam, / a charnel house."

Silt loam . . .

The day she and her father walked along the Mississippi River, he'd said, "These banks are pure silt loam." But what's "charnel house"? She types the phrase into the browser, opening the Webster Dictionary definition. Her blood chills as she reads. "The charnel house is a place of violent death, a bone-house, ossuary, morgue." At once, she closes the laptop. A rolling shudder tremors her body as though someone had doused her with ice water or, as Mom used to say, "someone just walked over your grave."

Rotting teeth, now a morgue . . . If she were superstitious, she'd be worried.

Rolling onto her side, she glances out the window at a view that always soothes. But tonight, dark, ominous clouds over Manhattan's skyline intensify her disquiet.

She closes her eyes, then opens them swiftly as the girl's bony face and hands infiltrate her mind. Pulling the sheet over her shoulder, she blanks the dream away with images of Marseille. She drifts to a place two stories high strung with bright string lights floating above a festive rooftop dinner. Soon, sleep carries her to Baton Rouge.

An herbal breeze infuses her nose. Brilliant yellow blossoms and baby-blue skies drift in her vision. Grass sweeps a cotton sundress outgrown years ago in a place she'd played as a child—a cluster of crabgrass, goldenrods, and wildflowers beyond her home. A familiar hum and squeak resonate nearby, drawing her gaze toward the dwelling ahead. She rises in disbelief, eyeing her humming mother swaying back and forth on the red-cedar porch swing.

"Mom?" Simone moves toward the yard calling, "Mom, you're here!"

The humming and creaking cease as she rises from the swing, her favorite cherry-print dress furling upward past her ankles. An inscrutable smile brightens her face as she strolls through the cobalt door, summoning her with her hand.

Simone hastens forward, struggling to reach the receding porch as the lengthening yard drags the house afar with each stride. The ground dips, caving, oscillating beneath unsteady feet, threatening to pluck her underground as soil peaks and valleys, the home shrinking unreachable.

"Mom, wait!"

"Hurry, child. I don't have much time," Mom hollers through the door, miles away.

Breathless, sprinting toward the porch, she spreads her rubbery arms, curling her fingers around the doorframe, pulling, bounding inside screaming, "Mom, where are you!?"

"In here, Moni. Hurry now," her sober tone rises.

Simone follows her voice and sweet aroma into the kitchen, startled by her loud hand clap. A cloud of flour disperses between them, hovering backward above her mother's head, never falling, flowing in reverse motion as she utters strange words.

"Rebmemer tahw I dlot uoy."

Drifting to the counter, Mom wipes flour on the scarlet apron, latticing narrow dough strips across sliced peaches, never lifting her gaze. Tears leak from her eyes, melting and glimmering on sugared spices. She carries the cobbler to the oven, the cloud above her head billowing behind her back. Cherries bounce and roll, changing and reassembling to peaches on the embroidered dress. From behind, her shoulders hitch in disjointed jerks with her peculiar expressions.

"Rebmemer tahw I dlot uoy."

"Mom, I don't understand."

She turns, white flour clouds winging at her shoulder blades, her eyes glassy pools, mouth an open dark chasm spewing peach pits from a black, forked tongue splitting into three limbs licking around her chest. Petals bloom pale, magenta, flaming pink. She clutches her heart with a terror-stained face, wailing, "Senob deirub woleb s'zehctan sffulb! Senob deirub woleb s'zehctan sffulb! Senob deirub woleb s'zehctan sffulb!"

Wild blossoms loop and absorb her bosom to foot.

Screaming and reaching through the floury mist, Simone swats at intoxicating posies, tugging arteriole branches, straining to free her blossomed figure. The kitchen shakes, stirring a cloud of powdery dust, elongating as blossoms shape to bony arms yanking her from reach.

"KooB fo wehttaM: retpahC neves: esreV neethgie," she screams, a dwindling floral speck vanishing in the distance.

"Mommmmmmm!" Simone calls out in her sleep, tears wetting her pillow as her mom's figure withers in the dream.

Forsaken souls rise at harvest,
Imparting offerings of history's horrors,
Oh, what bittersweet hymns of sorrow,
Below the bluffs of Natchez Trace.

ARRIVAL

BATON ROUGE, LOUISIANA

Simone peers out the narrow cabin window of the Boeing 747 winging toward Baton Rouge Metropolitan Airport, comforted at the nearness of her birthplace. On the last visit home, she and her father attended the Bayou Classic's football game between Southern University's Jaguars and Grambling State University's Tigers. A momentous occasion for the Doucet family and the state of Louisiana around Thanksgiving, more so for her father as staff director of Southern University's (SU) athletics department. In every respect he's devoted, attending every game. The profound loss of his favorite cheerleader has stifled the exhilaration, but they will carry Lily in their hearts and minds at every Bayou Classic.

She sighs, releasing unease that's lingered from four nights of frightful dreams and dampened the elation she would have felt for the Natchez assignment. It's been a month since she dreamt of her mother, and Simone had never experienced anything as horrific and bewildering as the alien words her mother had spewed. The angelic images floating around her body reassured Simone that her mother was in a heavenly place. But the peach pits rolling from her forked tongue were demonic. Resting her head on the seat, she wonders if images of the wraithlike girl were jumbled in with her mother's dream? The contiguous nightmares can't be a coincidence but must be connected. She shakes her head, positing that her mentioning her mother's peach cobbler to Bridgette had triggered the dream.

A ray of setting sun splits her periphery. She rolls her head toward the airplane window, gazing at low clouds melting through swift aluminum wings. After four nights of disturbed sleep, the airplane's drone and crystalline heavens lull her to a red-cedar porch swing on her family's Arcadian-style home in Southdowns Baton Rouge.

Rosaceae vines twist and slither through red-cedar rails, copious flexing tendrils rocking the porch swing to and fro, catching the beginning and tail end of words echoing beside her. Creepers round their waist, an umbilical cord binding them in place. Resounding words elucidate as Mom reads a leaf of paper between bible pages on her lap, softly and solemnly intoning, "Forsaken souls rise at harvest, imparting offerings of history's horrors. Oh, what bittersweet hymns of sorrow, below the bluffs of Natchez Trace . . ." She lifts the testament to her heart, voice elevating: "book of Matthew, chapter seven, verse eighteen." She leans over, kisses her cheek, and whispers, "Moni, tell her story . . ." Vines snap from their waists, snatching her breath, affecting a guttural gasp.

The plane hits an air pocket, jolting Simone awake. She gasps, clutches her heart, and touches her cold cheek.

"Are you OK?" the furrowed-browed man beside her asks.

"Um, yes, fine, thank you . . . Just a dream." She forces a smile and sits back in the seat, glancing out the window. The Book of Matthew: Chapter seven: Verse eighteen repeats in her mind. *What is she trying to tell me? She's not trying to prevent her from going to*

Natchez as her father assumed but guide her toward what she discovered.

The talk with her dad three days ago resurface, his tone elevated as she speaks of the dreams, the cryptic stanza, and the assignment in Natchez.

"Natchez, did you say Natchez, Mississippi?"

"Is something wrong?"

For an instant he grew quiet before replying, "Lily visited there right before . . . a month before she passed. Something rattled her in Natchez, but she refused to tell me what happened. She spoke of a poem her friend read to her. I believe it refers to the Devil's Punchbowl."

"What's the Devil's Punchbowl?"

"A forested basin below Natchez's bluffs. I've heard horrible tales of that place, atrocities that should never have happened."

"What happened?"

"I can't discuss this at work. But the stanza you spoke is from Lily's poem."

"Do you have it, Dad?"

"It remains where your mother left it, and that's where it will remain, between pages of her bible in the nightstand. We need to leave it be, Simone. I believe whatever happened to Lily in Natchez contributed to her heart attack. When she arrived back home, nightmares plagued her every sleepless night. She refused to go back to sleep, mumbling about those poor souls. Simone, there's a reason you're having these dreams. It sounds impossible, but your mother's reaching out to you. Don't ignore the dreams. I believe Lily wants to protect you from whatever she discovered in Natchez."

"Why didn't you tell me?"

"I thought it best to leave it be. There wasn't any reason to disturb you further. Simone, please don't take the assignment?"

"I'm not turning down another paycheck. Besides, I've already accepted the job. Don't worry. The B&B's safe. Nothing will happen. Dad, why did Mom go to Natchez?"

"Her childhood friend Ella took ill. Lily was there for support until her family arrived."

"Is she OK now?"

"Miraculously, her health improved a day after your Mom arrived. I guess Lily's healthy cooking healed her fast," he'd supposed, chuckling. "She told me Ella's fridge and cabinets were bare, so she went to the farmers' market in town. On her way back, she stopped alongside the road at a peach stand owned by an elderly gentleman who spoke in a strange dialect that sounded suspiciously like Gullah, an old slave dialect. She swore she'd never seen peaches so big and plump. When she asked which orchard grew the peaches, the man said they were the best peaches in Adams County and were grown behind his home. Lily couldn't stop talking about that darn intoxicating cobbler she made for Ella. She said they devoured the entire dish in one night. That same evening, the frightful girl visited Lily with horrible images of the Devil's Punchbowl. The dream plagued her until her death."

"Ladies and gentlemen, BTR has cleared us for landing at Baton Rouge. Please be seated," the pilot sounds from the speaker.

Simone positions the seat upright, buckles the seatbelt, and glances at the greenish-brown Mississippi River snaking through verdant cliffs, looking up and down the banks of Louisiana and Mississippi. Studying the outline, she tries to determine where the Devil's Punchbowl lies before the river slips past her view. Gradually, the plane glides over squared, russet terrain, freeways, industrial sites, tree-bordered homes, descends, and then taxis across the runway.

Several minutes later, the flight attendant announces over the intercom, "Welcome to Baton Rouge," the rest of her words muted by Simone's incessant reflections as she gathers her carry-on bag, moves through the aisle, and deplanes in rote fashion, arriving at the baggage conveyor. Retrieving her Samsonite, she heads toward Hertz and moments later exits BTR airport, actions performed in a mental fog. Since the first dream, she felt something undefinable attached to her soul, woke with her, followed her into conscious and unconscious reality, occupying her thoughts with unknowable compulsions.

Even as she drives through Baton Rouge Central Business District, an urge compels her to detour to her nearby home in the Southdowns' section and retrieve the poem from her mother's Bible in the bedside table drawer. But she imagines her superstitious father has locked it up and thrown away the key. She needs to get to the B&B and finish the assignment before visiting home.

On US 84 West, a destination sign points toward Natchez. She realizes she'd seen the sign many times on this road, but it held no significance until now. Nothing much about Natchez ever crossed her path growing up except for the occasional calls from Ella, mom's dearest friend, but she'd forgotten she lives in Natchez.

Ella . . .

She gave Mom the poem. Is she the poet? If not, she might know who wrote the verses. But she doesn't have her number or address. Years ago, she'd overheard Mom mention that Ella worked for the Museum of African History in her town. "Hmm . . ." she mumbles, tapping her fingers on the steering wheel. She could call her at work or call dad for her number, but he'd see right through her inquiry.

~

Simone had no problem finding the museum's telephone number on her cell phone browser. After several rings, a sluggish male voice answers, "Natchez Museum of African American History and Culture."

"Hello, may I speak with Ella Davis?"

"Ella Davis?"

"Yes."

"I don't recognize the name. Do you want the Natchez Museum of African American History and Culture?"

"Yes," she states with a lifted brow. "She's an employee."

"There's no Ella Davis at this museum."

Simone twists her lips. "Are you sure?"

"I'd recognize the name." His lethargic reply sounds as though the call staved off sleep or boredom.

"Ella Davis has been a museum employee for years. Can you check, please?"

"We have a small staff, but I'll check the directory." For a moment, paper rustles as he rifles through the employee register with a deep exhalation. "Nope," he states with a final paper flutter. "I'm sorry, Miss. Ella Davis isn't on the list."

"She has to be. Can I talk to someone else?"

"Just a moment. I'll connect you to the administrator."

Finally, she thinks, irritated.

Seconds later, a woman answers, "Cindy Wright."

"Hi, I hope you can help me. I'm looking for an employee, Ella Davis, but I was just informed she's not on the employee roster."

"Who am I speakin' to?" the chary administrator asks.

"Simone Doucet. I'm a family friend of Mrs. Davis."

"Ella retired a year ago."

"She did? I didn't know. Hmpf, well, that's a snag in my plan. I'm only in town for a week and hoped to see her. Do you have her home number on file?"

"That's private employee information. But you can reach Ella on Saturday at the museum. Since she retired, she volunteers once a week. Did you say your last name is Doucet?"

"I did."

"Are you related to Lily and Roderick Doucet?"

"Yes," Simone replies, startled to hear her parents' name from a stranger. "I'm their daughter. Do you know my parents?"

"No, not personally. I recognized the Doucet cognomen from the quarterly museum mailin' list. Your parents are regular patrons of the museum."

Simone wasn't aware of her parent's patronage but recalls her father's anxious, last-minute scramble every tax season to find charity receipts for tax write-offs. Once, she'd heard him ask Mom for the museum payments. She thought they'd visited a museum in Baton Rouge. "Yes, Mom and Ella were childhood friends."

"Were?"

"Mom passed away four months ago."

"Oh, dear! I'm so sorry to hear that. My deepest condolences."

"Thank you."

"Well, Ella became a good friend while she worked here. She often spoke of Lily during our conversations. I'm sure she'd love to hear your voice. Do you have a pen handy?"

"Um . . . just a second," she mumbles, reaching toward the dashboard for the mobile in the hands-free device. The car swerves. She grips and steadies the wheel. "Um, I'm driving and can't reach my mobile—"

"Give me your cell phone number. I'll text Ella's contact information."

At once, Simone rattles off her number, repeating it twice.

"Hold on one second . . . there we go. It just went through."

Simone's mobile chimes. "I got it. Cindy, thanks so much for your help."

"You bet. Please give my condolences to your father."

"I will. Thank you." Simone ends the call, perceiving

her parents donated to the museum to support Mom's lifelong friend. Hmm, how often did they visit the museum or Natchez?

To her bewilderment and recollection, Mom made occasional trips to Mississippi, but Ella never visited Baton Rouge. She'd met Ella only once, at her mom's funeral, but had heard her voice many times, as Mom and Ella were close and spoke on the phone often. She was but an intangible, high-pitched voice, not real in her world. This was one reason Simone never felt obliged to keep in touch after Lily's death. How might she react to a sudden inquisitive call concerning a mysterious poem four months after the funeral?

"What the . . ." Cars come to a complete stop with the traffic jam ahead. A police cruiser and ambulance sound behind, appearing in her rearview mirror, and speed past. If it's an accident, it might be a while before the roads clear. Blowing air through her lips and staring at the mobile on the dashboard, she reckons now's the perfect time to speak to Ella.

Inhaling deep, she dials Ella's number, exhaling when a familiar high-pitched voice answers with a rich southern brogue through the hands-free cell phone on the dashboard.

"Hello."

"Ella?" Simone asks, staring straight ahead at the road.

"Yes, who's this?"

"It's Simone, Lily's daughter."

"Simone? Dear Lord, what a surprise, sweetheart. Goodness gracious, I never thought I'd hear your voice again after losin' your mama. Is somethin' wrong, child? How's your papa doin'?"

"Oh, no, I'm sorry to alarm you. Nothing's wrong, and Dad's fine. It must be strange hearing from me out of the blue. I've meant to call sooner and apologize it's taken this long."

"Don't apologize. Lily told me about your job. I imagine your schedule's hectic flying around the world. All that matters is that you called."

"I landed at Baton Rouge airport an hour ago. I'm on my way to Natchez now for an assignment and thought I'd let you know I'm in town."

"Wonderful. You should stop on by the house. I can cook us somethin' to eat while we catch up."

"I'd love to, Ella, but I have to get to the B&B and check-in today. Perhaps tomorrow after I've settled in."

"Then I'll prepare a small meal while we talk. How about lunchtime?"

She imagines a table filled with buttery ice-laced cakes, crispy fried meats, thick gravies, Polk-weed salads, greens, and bread—southern favorites. Mom praised Ella's Mississippi Mud cake and sometimes brought slices home along with a basket of Ella's other baked goods, which she and Dad devoured to the last crumb. "No, please, don't go out of your way for me."

"It's no bother. I haven't cooked for anyone but myself since my husband passed, and the children all moved away. It will be a pleasure cookin' for someone else."

How lonely she must be without her family and closest friend. And how inconsiderate she's been, not calling since the funeral. "That sounds wonderful. Ella, something's been troubling me since I accepted the assignment."

"Oh? What is it, Moni?"

The nickname her mom used often, and one Ella adopted from her parents, induces simultaneous warmth and dread, evoking her mother's surreal appeal on the airplane. "Moni, tell her story."

"Moni, you there?"

"Oh, sorry, Ella."

"What's achin' you, child?"

"The thing is, I've been having unusual dreams of

Mom and a strange poem on Natchez. When dad heard the verse, he said the words are from a poem Mom received from you during her last visit. Do you recall the poem, Ella?"

"May I ask where you got the poem?" she asks swiftly, alarmed.

"I-It . . . this might sound bizarre, but the first verse just popped into my head, and the rest came to me in a dream."

"Oh . . ."

"Do you know the poet?"

"No, I wish to heavens I did," Ella replies with a long sigh and even longer pause. "The poem was given to me anonymously at the museum. Someone walked in and requested the program director, which was me at the time, receive the envelope. No name. No note. No return address. Just the poem. You sure Lily never read it to you?"

"No, I heard it for the first time four days ago in my dream. It's the oddest thing. The first line of the stanza came to me right before I accepted the assignment. Then that same night, I had a horrible dream."

"Was there a young gal with child in your dream?"

With child? She'd believed the bundle under the girl's skirt was peaches. She was pregnant . . . . "How did you know?"

"Where are you stayin', Moni?"

Simone's brows rise and furrow at Ella's skirting of the question. Why ask about the girl then overtly dodge her response? Her rudeness leaves her more than curious, but she doesn't press the issue just yet. "At Magnolia Sunrise Bed & Breakfast."

"Oh!" she responds sharply. "Out on the bluffs?" she asks in a lower pitch. "Near the cemetery?"

"Yes. Is something wrong?"

"Er, well, no . . . it's a lovely place. I reckon that's a good two miles from my home. We need to talk tomorrow, and you're more than welcome to stay here durin' your visit."

"Thanks, Ella, but part of my assignment is the B&B, so I'll need to remain there. But a visit for a few hours tomorrow is good. Oh, I don't have your address."

"Is this your cell phone number?"

"Yes."

"I'll text you the address and directions."

"Thanks . . ." Simone pauses, irked by her evasiveness and wanting answers to her earlier inquiry. "Ella, Dad said when Mom returned from visiting you, she had horrible dreams and couldn't sleep. He believes the dreams and poems contributed to her heart attack. Did she mention the dreams before her death?"

"Moni, I'll clarify everything tomorrow."

Simone narrows her eyes and holds her tongue. "OK."

"I can't wait to see you, child."

"Me too, Ella. Tomorrow at noon, then."

"I'll be here, good Lord willin' and the creek don't rise."

Simone chuckles at a southern saying she hasn't heard in years. "All right, Ella." She ends the call with a genuine laugh she hasn't had in days, but it quickly fades as worry floods her mind again.

Ahead, policemen motion cars off the freeway to another ramp. Simone follows the other vehicles onto a scenic route to Natchez. Carefully watching road signs, she ruminates over the abrupt change in Ella's tone at the mention of the poem. Her evasiveness sends greater dread through her mind. Something sinister is behind that poem. Maybe she should listen to Dad and leave it be. But the dreams won't let her do so.

Beware the crag on summer eves,
She arrives, aggrieved,
Arms replete with plummy treasures.
Oh, how tempting, succulent, sweet,
Yet, wicked to the pitted marrow.
One bite, she'll reveal
A grim genesis of horrors,
Skeletal antiquity,
Deeply seeded,
Root-to-leaf fodder,
For the Devil's harvest,
Below the bluffs of Natchez Trace.

MAGNOLIA SUNRISE

NATCHEZ, MISSISSIPPI

Natchez's sweltering heat hangs heavy in the air with no reprieve from muggy breezes, just more humidity only an air conditioner relieves. Seated behind the rental car's chilly vents, Simone pays little heed to the scorching weather, consumed with unpleasant dreams and bothersome queries which subdue the venture's novelty and excitement. Ominous vibes persist from Brooklyn like a Geiger counter needle drifting further right toward an unknown threat the closer she gets to the B&B.

"Moni, tell her story . . ."

"Who and what story, Mom?" she queries under her breath, thumping her hand into the wheel. "Is it about Natchez?"

She dips her head shoulder to shoulder, rubs her stiff neck with a loud exhalation, and pushes slipped sunglasses atop her nose. To the right and left of the lane, behind towering oaks, pecan, and magnolia trees, postbellum plantations, once bordered by lucrative cotton and tobacco fields and slave shanties during the antebellum era, roll past her rose-tinted view.

Ahead, on Cemetery Road, an open wrought-iron gate flanked by two white pillars and low red brick walls marks the entrance to Natchez National Cemetery.

She wonders about Bridgette's honeymoon destination choice. This is not the magazine's typical wedding get-away. Newlyweds might be horror-struck to learn rows and rows of graves border the B&B, unless a haunted retreat is what they seek. Regardless, she's curious to see the Turning Angel effigy described on the city's website. With the sun dimming over the massive necropolis, it's much too eerie to explore alone. She'll brave the cemetery another day on Natchez's haunted horse-and-buggy ghost tour.

Per Parker's driving directions, she slows the car past the gate, as the B&B is located two houses north of the graveyard. Atop steep forested bluffs sit private homes on both sides of the winding, narrow two-lane road. Do homeowners fear that one day the craggy sandstone walls will give way, sucking their properties into the swampy depths below?

Past a large Greek Revival-style home, the white facade of a grand antebellum Victorian wavers through trees. Magnolia Sunrise Bed-and-Breakfast sits far off the road, cloistered behind a creepy live oak with knotted branches sweeping the ground and a dark-green triangular magnolia tree. Simone steers the car onto the long private driveway curving behind the B&B, parking in the rear beside five vehicles. A whiff of magnolia's citrus honey and fragrant honeysuckles over-power fresh-mowed grass and brackish delta breezes coming off the river when she exits the rental.

As she approaches the stone pathway, a thirtyish-looking man of average stature and build wearing white crepe drawstring pants, a navy Polo T-shirt, and flip-flops rises from a regal wicker rocker.

"Simone?" he asks, stepping off the porch with a hop in his walk.

"Yes. Parker?"

A Duchenne smile explodes across his face, feathers his bright eyes, and brackets fine lines around his gracile lips. His hands fly from his pockets, held aloft. "Girl, where you been?" he asks in an overly familiar twang as if they're old friends, enfolding her in a swift embrace.

Simone flinches then stiffens in his gentle squeeze. Does he greet every guest with such exuberant southern charm and call an utter stranger girl? His familiarity might displeasure others. But she's sure their mutual friendship with Bridgette warranted the hug.

Parker releases his arms, steps back, and inserts his hands in his pants pockets while probing her face with a charming grin. "We expected you an hour ago for supper."

She fuses her agape lips, imparting a rueful grimace. "I was hoping to arrive in time for dinner, but an accident on US 84 snarled traffic. Patrol rerouted cars to the scenic roads, which took more time, but I enjoyed views of historic homes."

"Ahhh, lost in the view. I hope you didn't miss the turnoff admiring the scenery." He chortles in jest.

Simone grins at his playfulness. "Nah, despite the detour, I found the house without a hitch, given your easy-to-follow directions."

Parker's kind baby-blue eyes narrow beneath thick curly eyelashes, contrasting masculine facial features in a peculiar but appealing way. "I bet you're tuckered from the trip. Let's get you into the AC."

Now she understands why this spirited, unpretentious man with infectious energy appealed to Bridgette. From the bounce of his hips to his corn-silk hair he exudes perkiness.

"Bridge spoke fondly of you, and you're just as stunning as she said."

"Oh, thank you. Brigette's the best. She spoke highly of you and Amelia, too," Simone replies, tearing her long stare from his enviable lashes and tugging at the Samsonite.

"I got that."

"Um, oh, no, I . . ." Before she can object, he lifts the luggage off the ground, the muscles of his shoulder taut beneath the polo shirt as he carries rather than rolls it through the door. "Thank you," she replies, following him inside the home.

"I'm afraid Amelia's traveling a few days, but she should be back before you leave. We have five couples for the week: two honeymooners and three couples visiting from various states," he explains, setting the luggage on the floor. "Welcome to our charming home."

"Spectacular," Simone praises, turning in circles and gawking at the stunning architecture, rich decor, spiraling staircase, and the large room beyond the foyer. Chandeliers sparkle off brilliant white walls and shiny cypress wood floors. The chic and modern black-and-white theme showcased throughout the space looks as if someone doused a paintbrush in chocolate and flecked it over the white home. Ebony finials and fittings, charcoal picture frames, glossy onyx railings along eggshell stairs, and graphite metal lanterns placed around the home contrast with the overall whiteness of the furniture and walls.

"Amelia's the interior designer and artistic one in the family. She strove to mix contemporary southern elegance with a touch of British décor."

"I always assumed the south adopted interior design from early British settlers. But I guess I'm wrong."

"Interior design isn't my forte, but you could learn a lesson or two from my British wife."

"I thought you both were Natchez natives."

"I was born here but lived abroad for many years. Amelia is London born. We both met Bridgette at university and have remained friends since graduation."

"Ah, I see."

"Your suite's this way, on the south-western end of the home with sweeping vistas of Miss-Lou."

Simone grins. "Miss-Lou. It's been a long time since I've heard that term."

"I figured a Baton Rouge native knows the river divide between Mississippi and Louisiana as good old Miss-Lou."

"Hmm," Simone mutters, narrowing one eye. "I see Bridgette sent my dossier before my assignment began," she says with a frivolous grin.

Parker's chortle rings around the foyer. "A page or two. She had only great praises for you. She said you're a wonderful writer, too good for a travel magazine."

"Dear me, such exalts. I'm blushing," she states with humor, invoking an old twang. "Yep, I'm Louisiana bred but left soon after college. Brooklyn's my home now, between travels for work. But I find my way home every year for the holidays."

"One can never leave their roots for too long."

The simple comment reflects wisdom and has a poignant tone, revealing personal experience that resonates true for Simone. She nods in agreement and follows him through a long gallery of portraits. Their sandals echo around the space, flip-flopping to a silent pause before the paintings.

At a distance from the wall, several gold-fringed Victorian chairs with crimson cushions border the windowless space, reminiscent of a sitting room in a museum, positioned in front of a wall of paintings that belong on a prominent surface. Perhaps they hung in a grander space years ago.

Large, gilded frames enclose pictures of Magnolia Sunrise Plantation during the 1800s and images of a striking family. A handsome blond man dressed in a navy-blue cutaway coat with tails and breeches tucked into boots stands beside an attractive woman sitting in what appears to be the same chair as the one behind Simone. Blonde ringlets fall around sharp features, piercing sky-blue eyes, and tight lips. A white-and-gold brooch accentuates her elegant neck. Two twin boys stand at her side, leaning into the folds of her voluminous velvet lilac hoop skirt. The children possess prominent blue eyes and a deep tan, though their reddish-brown curls display a striking contrast to their parent's blond strands.

Drawn to a smaller portrait alongside the others, she inches closer to the image of a pubescent slave girl with a diffident smile and the glare of a lioness cradling two ivory-gowned Caucasian infants on her lap as though they came from her womb. Why paint just one girl? Weren't there many slaves at Magnolia Sunrise Plantation? Simone's gaze locks on the girl's youthful eyes tightened in spite, in anger. Her hair painted a burnished brown, eyes walnut-colored beneath long, lush lashes. Where has she seen . . .

"This is Remembrance Hall. Paintings of the original owners have graced these walls since the beginning. Amelia insisted on keeping them. I was and still am ambivalent about venerating slaveowners. But this was their home. We maintained the original fixtures in this room, except for the hideous wallpaper. Those are original Louis XV chairs, and the only original furniture you'll find in the home, besides Blackamoor statues we kept in each bathroom." He pauses, noticing Simone's furrowed gaze as she looks at the painting of the slave girl. "I hope the pictures and the home's atrocious past don't offend you?"

"Huh, um, no . . . " His abrupt question startles, leaving her disinclined to voice genuine sentiment. Nor should she on an assignment. *"Always be respectful. Shine with kindness, not bitterness."* Her mother's disciplines emerge, prompting her next response. "Slavery is a dark and unfortunate part of Magnolia's history, not its present reality. You can't change the past." Simone grimaces at the clichéd maxim's utter triteness. But in a non-work-related setting, a candid response might have ensued. A home where a slaveowner's disdain instilled fear and debased subordinates might unnerve any person of color.

Parker smiles and nods his head with unswerving graciousness. But the diminished whites of his eyes affirm he's well aware of her immediate perception.

"To be honest, the home's history is bothersome. It's not something one wishes away or ignores. To do so negates my people's suffering. And I can't. But I'm not stuck in the past and I do not harbor hatred. I just hope it's a lesson people consider for a better future." Simone seldom thinks of her color, hoping others see her as a human being first and foremost. However, standing in the gallery next to Parker, she's more aware than ever. History whispers through Magnolia, reminding her she would have walked these halls as a servant centuries ago.

"Thank you for being honest. The home's history is a constant struggle for me. That young girl there," he says, pointing at the painting, "played a crucial role in this house. Records show they purchased her from the slave market at Forks of the Road just outside of town where Natchez Trace ends."

"Oh, I saw the historical marker on entering the city." Something made her park the car at the side of the road and venture to the sign, the only symbol marking the site of an auction block across which many slaves passed as they were sold to plantations in the area. "So much history in Natchez," she states, staring at the girl again. "She was beautiful."

"Her name was Delphine. She was more than a servant at Magnolia Sunrise." He turns and points at the image of the blonde woman with the angular face and cutting eyes. "Lorelei Randolph, the owner's wife, was consumptive, weak, and bedridden with tuberculosis a year before her death. Delphine oversaw the house with her mother, Josephine, known as Josie to the owners.

Amelia and I researched Delphine's history when we discovered the painting in an upstairs room closet. A room we understand she stayed in when she was nursing Lorelei's babies—"

"A wet nurse?"

"Yes, that's a correct epithet. Well, we decided her painting belongs right beside the others after learning of her influential role at Magnolia Sunrise."

"What happened to her?"

Parker draws a slow, troubled breath and narrows his gaze on the painting as though expecting the girl to answer. He releases a breath and states, "Delphine fled the plantation during the Civil War with her brother, Benoit, and headed north with other slaves from surrounding plantations. We tried but couldn't trace her whereabouts after the war. But official army records revealed her brother joined Grant's black infantry and died June 1864 fighting in the Battle of Petersburg."

"Oh . . ." Investing time and energy researching this girl's past strikes her as odd. She's not an ancestor. Of what importance is she to them other than as a past servant of the home, a wet nurse to her master's children?

Parker tips his head right, signaling her to follow. "The suite lies on the south-western end, a distance from other rooms. Perfect for honeymooners seeking privacy," he explains in a drawl as slow as his saunter.

Simone continues behind Parker's easy-going pace, head sideways, staring at the slave girl's spiteful eyes until they traverse the gallery. Entering a long passage with a lengthy cream-and-silver console adjoined by two side chairs beneath a large photo of present-day Magnolia Sunrise, they arrive at her suite.

"Here we go." He opens the door. "Welcome to the Bluff-side suite."

Simone clasps her mouth with a chilling recognition, stifling the terror rising in her throat. At once, she checks her wits in silence behind Parker, relieved he's oblivious to a fright she could not explain. The disturbing images that plagued her unrelentingly four nights in a row originated here. Though hazy in her dream, she recognizes the spacious lounge adjoining a large bedroom with two tall windows lining one wall. Open drapes display a garden and a brilliant sunset. Next to the windows, familiar French doors lead to a patio. *It's the same room*, she confirms, considering a retreat to the car and never returning.

"A private patio and en suite bath border the bedroom. Although you're not a honeymooner, we provided the exact treatment we give every newlywed couple." Parker's voice resounds through a mental haze as he places the Samsonite in the bedroom.

A disconnect between her brain and feet, two opposing forces, cause Simone to dither at the door. She swallows the dreadful lump in her throat and tries to gather courage when another force propels her forward into a dream, now a reality.

Glass-paneled French doors that mirrored a full moon in her dream squeal open, slinging a sultry breeze into the air-conditioned room as Parker strides into the stone-tiled yard.

"The patio offers private dining and a fantastic view."

Flashes of the eerie girl and her rolling bounty overshadow Parker's voice. Simone pauses in astonishment near the high four-poster bed with white canopy bed curtains, glaring at the Hadleigh bed step she'd descended in her dream. Everything's the same, even the gift basket, complimentary champagne on the nightstand, bouquets of roses, and several assorted flower vases around the suite. A room staged for romance, not fear. None of which calms her anxiousness.

She's never seen this place before today. How could she dream it? Were they premonitions, omens of something evil? Was Mom trying to warn her? Certainly not, she thinks, recalling images of the dream and Lily's plea. She wants her to *tell her story*.

She releases a breath and the tight grip on her handbag, considering asking Parker for another room. *I can't. It's rude, not to mention odd and suspicious when they've given her the best suite in the home. Besides, there's only one vacancy, the room adjoining Amelia and Parker's suite.*

On the patio, a small firepit, umbrella-covered table, and a stone path leads to the garden's edge, just as in her dream. It's real. The drag of chains on stones reverberates in her memory. A chimera of images—bloody peaches, fallen teeth, deep tar sockets—sour her expression.

Parker pivots toward her, frowning. "Are you OK?"

Expressive, never able to hide emotions, she seldom holds back, not that she can, unless her response is inappropriate, hurtful, or in this case, inexplicable. How could she explain a dream she doesn't understand herself? Besides, she's here for work, not to divulge or uncover what she's experiencing. But maybe it's connected. Delving into the home's history will help her write a more compelling article. To allay Parker's momentary concern, she forces a smile and replies with several quick nods, afraid her voice will give away her fear.

"You looked horrified a minute ago."

"Mere astonishment," she lies with a nervous titter. "What a well-designed patio and the perfect place to view the river and magnificent sunset," she says with exaggerated exuberance, looking at the picturesque horizon.

"From this angle, sunsets splay breathtaking, colorful ribbons over the river most evenings." Parker walks toward the garden and points at the fenced hedgerow. "Just a precaution. We created the garden to prevent guests from wandering too near the edge. There's a lethal drop beyond the fence."

Simone's pulse races. The shrubbery incites images of a peach rolling to her feet and the girl's bony hand. It's the same bush. But there wasn't a fence in her dream.

"What's below the bluff?"

"A bowl-shaped gulch with a deadly history."

"Oh? Deadly?"

Parker sighs and cups his chin in his hand with a pensive stare. "Well, many folktales purport horrible deeds happened over the years. Many myths, a few, real. Other tales revolve around peach orchards that grow there, but thick woods, gators, and other critters make it a dangerous place to venture."

Dangerous place to venture . . . Is it the place Dad mentioned? Simone narrows her eyes, strolls toward the spicy-smelling sweet shrub and touches the wine-colored blossoms, recalling the rolling peach and the girl's infectious fingernails. She rubs her arm with a cringe. What happened in that gulch? Is it what the girl wants her to see? Instincts tell her something wicked occurred beyond the hedgerow where trees steeple to a sharp, tangled descent. "Is it the Devil's Punchbowl?"

"Yes, you're right, but it lies closer to the cemetery across the way."

"What a coincidence. I just learned it exists a few days ago. What happened there?"

"What hasn't happened in the bowl?" he states wryly with a heavy sigh, pausing in thought. "Well . . ." He pivots and scans the wooded decline beyond the bluff, turning around with haunted baby blues. "I shouldn't fill your head with tales your first night. That bowl's got layers of history too deep to explain. You need to unwind and enjoy the evening," he says, leading her back inside the suite. "Oh, I'm afraid you'll be eating alone as guests finished thirty minutes ago. But you're more than welcome to use the dining room, or do you prefer your suite?"

I prefer a room that doesn't freak me out, she thinks. "Dinner in my suite's fine. You're right. I should relax from the long trip. But I look forward to eating with your guests tomorrow."

A grin lightens the inscrutable darkness that crept into his face moments ago. "As you wish. Dinner in your suite, coming right up." He strolls toward a table set for two in the lounge by the sofa. "Lacy, our chef, will leave the tray here on the table." Sincerity warms his eyes. "Simone, any friend of Bridgette's is a friend of mine and Amelia's. If you need anything, just ask."

Simone follows him to the entrance, ready to inquire about the poem, but immediately changes her mind given his reluctance a moment ago. "Despite my comment on the plantation's history, I'm honored to be a guest in your magnificent home."

"Simone, you're always welcome at Magnolia Sunrise." He grins and closes the door with the same spiritedness with which he'd greeted her.

When the lock clicks, she roots to the spot, staring at the deluxe dreaded room, unable to shed ominous vibes. "Get a grip. You've got work to do. Nothing will happen," she mumbles, wandering toward the patio, shutting the door, and shuttering the view. But the impressions that followed from her dreams rally greater in this place, shown to her many times in dreams.

~

Despite the unease she feels in the room, Simone wolfs down a whole plate of tasty rosemary-sage-seasoned swordfish and grilled veggies, a spring salad with slivers of avocado, a big slice of decadent chocolate rum cake, and two glasses of chilled complimentary champagne. Her imaginary husband shares an invisible plate, silliness she condones whenever she is on assignment.

She wonders why her illusory husband always assumes her roommate Mitchell's face.

Now on her third goblet, Simone finds the sparkling wine quells anxiety and lights a warm tingle in her spirit. She begins a routine staged for every assignment, setting up a workspace of necessities placed side by side on the lounge table: laptop, pad and pen, recharger, a personal hotspot, and the last photo taken with her parents at the Bayou Classic three years before. As with each article, she writes a brief paragraph recounting the trip from the airport, first impressions of Natchez, Magnolia Sunrise, and the charming host. With greater detail, she depicts the romantic suite, amenities, and five-star dinner before the alcohol dulls her brain and fear overshadows the pleasant buzz again.

Dazed, she stares at the computer screen and slowly types "Devil's Punchbowl" with the image of Delphine's painting in her mind. She is goaded by another energy, one that wants her to express genuine emotions about this place.

"No, not in this article." Her instincts poke harder. There is another narrative to be told.

Moni, tell her story.

The incessant supplication has echoed nonstop since her flight. Who is this elusive she? Simone queries her brain, pausing on the specter in her dream.

"Is it her?" she asks, staring at her mother's picture on the table.

At once, she powers off the laptop and stares at daylight diminishing beyond slit curtains, expecting the wraith to creep around the house and through the patio door with peaches. She strolls toward the window and peers past the garden fence, fixing her gaze over treetops descending into the unfathomable gulch, picturing peach orchards ripe for harvest.

Coincidence?

The Devil's Punchbowl's proximity to the B&B, the

dreams, and her mother's death are not coincidental but related. Her father, Ella, and Parker are close-mouthed for a reason. But the strange expression on Parker's face after her inquiry piqued her interest. She glances at the bedroom's angle. "Only a yard away," she mumbles, discerning the nearness of the bluff.

An uncomfortable silence envelops the suite. No footsteps, not even echoing voices, only the giddy rush of champagne-laced blood pulsing in her ears. The stridulous chirping of faraway crickets, icy whispers from the air conditioner, and slight sounds, otherwise unnoticeable, amplify. And forthwith, as though someone read her thoughts, a remote door opens and closes somewhere in the house. Faint chatter emerges on the main level, growing more distant, a soft babble beyond the gallery, yet a comfort.

"Simone, you're ridiculous. Dreams aren't real," she mutters, strolling toward the bed, undressing, sauntering in her bare skin into the adjacent bath with multiple images of her body, back, front, side, surrounding the space like a funhouse in an amusement park. *How naughty*, she thinks, catching her backside and imagining newlyweds' sexy deeds in this space. She retrieves a towel from the built-in wall cabinet and turns toward the tub.

"Ah!" Simone gasps in horror, clutching her chest, losing the cloth to the floor. "Jesus, give your guest a heart attack, will ya," she mumbles, picking up the towel. "What the heck are you?" she asks the life-size, jet-black statue standing over the tub. The effigy of a slave woman wearing an African-styled toga draped from one shoulder to her feet looks at her with big bronze eyes, the whites bright in contrast to her jet-black skin. An air of servile civility shines in her toothy grin. Large bronze hoop earrings hang from her lobes; a magnificent choker wraps her neck. One ornate arm arches above her head, holding a gilded bowl, while the second arm extends forward, offering clean, folded towels. The startling Blackamoor Parker mentioned epitomizes servitude.

Why keep a symbol of slavery, knowing it might offend guests? But the home's historic, and the Blackamoor a relevant bygone relic. Perhaps Parker means to convey the servant's significance to Magnolia Sunrise.

Simone steps into the center of the room, noticing the same black-and-white theme throughout the opulent bathroom: white marble walls, black polished floor tiles, dark granite counters, alabaster ceramic double sinks, and the showpiece, a deep ivory claw-foot tub across from a walk-in shower. Lit votive candles border the tub on an adjoining shelf. Is the black-and-white theme a metaphor for the home's history?

She removes a bottle of Magnolia Sunrise bubble bath from a basket on the floor overflowing with various spa treatments. Turning on the faucet, she pours four too many caps of the floral-scented liquid into the stream.

The foamy bath caresses her in velvet warmth as she slides into the tub closing her eyes, soothed for the moment. The only sound is water lapping between her thighs as she peddles her knees up and down several times. Suds meet her chin as she sinks lower, placing a wet bath cloth over her eyelids.

Craaacck!

Pop!

The washcloth flies from her face over the tub, landing with a splat when she jerks toward the crackling cabinet. "Calm down . . . it's just moisture settling in the wood," she mutters with a nervous titter, leaving the cloth on the floor. She breathes deep, trying to achieve the same peace she'd felt a minute ago, but her heart races. At once, overhead lights dim, and the AC's drone grows fainter. The air grows heavy, quieter.

Her skin prickles in alarm as she inches her spine up

the curved bathtub. The presence she'd sensed in the brownstone unnerves her again. Gooseflesh covers her wet skin. Afraid to glance around, she clutches the edge of the tub and glares into the wide mirror over the sink, studying the spot at her rear beyond the bathroom door. Although her instincts perceive something behind her, the mirror belies her senses. Nothing reflects in the glass.

The odorous dampness she'd smelled four days ago overpowers, a vile sweetness. Simone shoots upright, sending water sloshing over the rim. Alert to a change in the room, she fixes her gaze on the mirror ahead.

A rumble sounds from the rear, growing louder, nearing her backside. Every muscle clench in an icy brace as she rolls her eyes sideways as a peach rattles past the tub and comes to rest under the counter.

It's not real.

She closes her eyes, willing it away, hoping it's gone on the count of five.

One. Two. Three. Four. Five.

The steadfast peach emerges through narrowed eyes under the counter, just as red and plump as in her dream. Something rustles behind her back. She freezes with shallow breath. Only her gaze moves to a pale, wavering configuration in the mirror. The translucent image is not a figment of her mind. She's there.

Frightened, Simone grips the rims, leans forward, reaching for the Blackamoor's outstretched hand for support. Her feet slide on the gelled bubble bath, crashing her back into the tub with a rolling splash and splattering water over the lip of the tub and into her mouth, gurgling her gasp. She pivots her head, glances over her shoulder at the swift-moving entity. Adrenaline fires her feet and hands hard against the enamel base and rim, propelling her body forward as the fast-approaching figure in the glass launches toward her.

The girl whooshes forward, a spear of air bursting

through Simone's backside, fusing with her flesh, claiming strength in every muscle as she slumps back into the water. A weight pins her to the ceramic tub, seizing her mind and restraining her voice as she struggles to break free. The girl's vaporous image rises from Simone, hovering over her, arms extended, palms holding her immobile.

Her bony form quivers, transforming.

Scabs along the girls face and chest shed to smooth brown skin. Mud drips from her hair revealing reddish-brown strands, coiling her girlish face. Her breasts and lifeless belly swell with milk and a phantom child. Her agape mouth spills silt loam snaking around her slender throat, sliding beneath her collarbone, a cascading ribbon entwined with breast milk, white and black, burying Simone shoulder to feet.

The girl's neck arches with an elongated wheeze coursing through her renewed mortal image. Her spine contorts; her head snaps back, dropping toward Simone. Chestnut threads weave and roll in hollow sockets, almond slits with curling lashes.

A captive to her spellbinding glare, Simone recognizes the defiant stare.

Delphine!

A marionette under her control, Simone's lips move, giving voice to Delphine's words.

"See me. See my horror."

Darkness clouds Simone's eyes, adhered to the girl's hypnotic gaze, transporting her to another time.

When Sumter thundered, plantations shuttered,
Relented barbarous tricentennial bondage,
Jubilant cries of freedom followed,
'til Union Armies hollered, halt,
Thwarting thousand's glory walk.
Detained, rerouted, entrapped, encamped on
     banks,
Flesh and bone buried where they sank.
Oh, what spoilage stains the bowl-shaped gulch,
Below the bluffs of Natchez Trace.

DELPHINE

1863, MAGNOLIA SUNRISE PLANTATION

MASSA RANDOLPH'S BOOTS CRUNCH ALONG SLAVE ROW'S
dirt path, growing silent in front of the cabin. Maw ambles to the window and gazes into the murky yard at his
still shadow, fearful of what's brought him out so late at
night. She prays he'll keep on straight to the main
house, but soil crunches beneath boots again, growing
closer.

"Dat bastard, not my child," Maw mumbles, moving
from the window as his boots stomp up steps and
across the porch.

The door bursts opened.

Maw jumps in front of the rocking chair, shoved
aside by Massa's strong hand, her petite frame colliding
with the wall.

Before Delphine can move, Massa yanks the baby
from her jiggling nipple and pulls her from the rocker
through the door, her leaking bosom exposed and Maw
chasing behind them.

"Massa Henry, please, she juz a child."

"Delphine ain't no child no moe, Josie. She ole
'nough to have babies. Now go on in the house. Lorelei
will take care of her."

Through blinding tears, Delphine peers back at Maw

cradling her newborn wailing for her milk, her nipples still atingle from her suckle. She glowers up at his stern face. He's a monster! No sympathy for her hungry baby or care that her open dress hangs off her shoulder. She stretches the moist frock over her tender, naked breast as Massa wrenches her across the yard.

"Gal, don't be prideful. You may be thirteen, but you got a woman's body. You no child no moe, you hear?"

She nods and glances at her bare feet tripping over each other, struggling to keep up with Massa's long-booted strides.

"Those tits ain't for maskin'. Now that Lorelei's hours from givin' birth, that milk belongs to her infants to feed as long as it takes."

"My babe needs feedin', Massa."

"I reckon with two breasts, you'll feed 'em both, but Miss Lorelei's newborn gets priority to that suck. Understand?"

"Yes, Massa."

Delphine trembles as they enter the home and climb the stairs to Massa's bedroom, growing closer to the pregnant Missus. Lorelei's glare made her weep as a child and cringe at horrific stories of servant's lashings and scaldings at her hands. "A monster lurks in her soul," she'd been told by Maw. "Lorelei got an evil streak. Her beauty's deceivin'. Dat sunny blonde hair, icy blue eyes, delicate pale features run skin deep, but her blood's moe toxic than a wolfsbane flower. Be careful 'round her, Delphine."

Chatter in the slave quarters was that Missus Lorelei asks for a young wet nurse, a gal who'd just given birth to nurse her infant. Delphine couldn't hide her belly's bulge from Massa, her child's father. She suspected he'd come seeking her.

Months ago, when Maw worked in the main house cooking as she did most days, he trapped and pinned her to the ground beneath a row of cornstalks in Maw's garden and pressed his hand hard to her mouth, muting her squeals. He did to her that awful thing a stallion did to a mare in the stables. After he had his way with her, he pulled up his pants and yelled, "Stop yo cryin' and get back in the cabin, gal." Later, bruised and balled up on her bed, Maw nursed her bruises and moaned in anger when she saw blood between her thighs.

"Youse a woman now. Don't fight Massa. Give him wat he needs. Youse know no pain." At her side, she opened a basket where she stored her herbal medicines and said, "Use dis after Massa has his ways. The cocklebur roots and bluestone stops da babies from comin'."

At seven, she saw him do the same to Maw. She woke to hushed groans in her corner bunk, watching, afraid beneath the blanket. When he dressed and left, Maw wept into her pillow so she couldn't hear. It happened more than once; each time she cried, hiding her suffering at daylight. She'd never asked what Massa did to her in bed. Now she knows her pain.

The day she and Maw got wind Missus Lorelei was scouting for a lactating gal to suckle her newborn, she prayed she'd find someone else. Tonight, when Massa entered the cabin, she nearly screamed, wanting to escape with her child attached to her nipple.

Being at Missus Lorelei's beck and call, she's bound to anger her. She's as frightening as a snake when upset, hissing harsh words or whipping servants as she'd done with the last girl, stripping and lashing her in front of everyone. But if she gives Missus what she needs, they'd let her leave and see her child again. She can't stand Missus's sly eyes watching as the newborn suckles her breast for days. Weeks. Months. A year. Until the baby desires no more milk.

~

One stillbirth and several miscarriages sent Lorelei into an obsessive delirium to get a baby by any means, a craze Delphine suffered for two years at Massa's pleasure and Missus's needs. She bore twins conceived from Massa's seed. Infants easily mistaken for Lorelei's blood, with blue eyes and fair skin. Russet curls, thick eyelashes, and full lips are the only hint they came from Delphine's womb. With Lorelei's wish for more children in the house, Delphine finds herself with child again, one she won't hand over this time.

Dey can't have another.

Delphine peers outside the nursery window at Slave Row. Hidden underneath corn stalks and turnip leaves in the small garden behind Maw's cabin lies a cloth satchel stuffed with items for her escape from Magnolia. News of emancipation reached plantations when Union soldiers marched into town and voiced their freedom. Jubilant cries and spirited dancing flowed through the slave quarters. She feared Massa's whip on their flesh till she'd heard the words the Union soldiers spoke.

Deys free . . . She's free.

Days and weeks later, slaves deserted their shanties. Many, too fearful of what awaited up north, and others too old or wanting the salary Massa promised them as freed servants, remained at Magnolia. She should've left when others fled days after they heard talk of freedom.

If it weren't for her babies, she'd have run off the moment soldiers rode into town declaring their emancipation. Massa Henry and Missus Lorelei lied to her and the others, promising they'd pay a salary if they stayed. She'd be better off up north than here as chattel to Massa and Missus's whims.

Maw refuses to leave and insists on keeping Delphine's firstborn. The child's more hers since Massa took Delphine away from her child and locked her in the main house, away from other servants when she's thick with a child. No one knows she carried twins and carries another babe now. Though she's pained to leave her babies, they're better off with Massa raised as their young 'uns.

Delphine jerks her head around when the nursery's doorknob twists.

He's too early! Lawd's testin' my will.

The door opens as she steps from the window.

Massa creeps on silent feet into the room, making his nightly visit. Her body has grown to expect him. Just as her nipples leak when she hears the babies' crying, her loins moisten minutes before Massa visits, as if she senses his manly needs. She's only ever known female pleasures with Massa, no other man, and suspects he desires her more than Missus, as his touch gentles now and his mouth finds hers often and lingers long. Where before she'd squirmed with hatred, now she allows his every need.

Maw was right. When she submits to Massa without a struggle, he gives her pleasure and grants her wishes, hidden from Missus. Many times, while Missus Lorelei lay in a laudanum-induced sleep, he'd allowed her to visit Maw and her firstborn. When she asked a year ago, he'd shown her how to read and write, her body a bargain for knowledge. Massa brought her children's books hidden from Missus under a loose floorboard beneath her bed. In a year, she'd learned them all, stories that offered solace as she read in a hush while the babies nursed.

Massa said she could earn two-hundred and fifty cents when she wrote a full sentence. When she did, he placed a shiny gold coin, a quarter eagle, in her palm. Money seldom crosses her path. Only on rare occasions when Missus reaches into her well-guarded silk crochet purse on the nightstand for coins to pay Doc for the laudanum or give to servants to buy food in town. Ignorant of the worth of coins or bills, she supposed two dollars and fifty cents more than enough to buy food up north.

North ...

She'd hoped to escape Magnolia two hours before Massa's midnight arrival. Now her only chance to leave is while he sleeps beside her. Delphine moves toward the slumbering twins, eyes misty as she suffers a look. Their faces always comfort her before Massa begins to grope. After tonight, she won't see her babies again. If she could journey north with them on her back, she would. But they're much too little to travel dangerous trails. Massa's growing affection for his babies eases her worry. The twins are better off with their poppa. And Missus will be glad to be rid of her and have them to herself.

She leans over and slides her finger between the mattress and the walnut wood frame, running her fingers across carved words concealed on the bottom rail. The first sentence she'd ever written left for others to discover.

The twins were born to Delphine Randolph in 1862.

When Missus slapped her face and called her a negroid ninny, she carved out her anger in furious digs and jabs, wishing it the Missus's flesh. No one knows that the words exist here, not even the man who taught her letters and numbers. She prays one day someone will discover the truth about the children. She made sure they would. She'd crawled beneath the Dutch box bed where she sleeps with a lantern and carved "The twins were born to Delphine Randolph in 1862" into a wooden plank with Missus's expensive silver butter knife. She figures as long as the house stands, the words will exist for someone to read long after Missus's bones are dried and brittle in the ground.

Delphine rubs the watery blur from her eyes and stares at the soothing yellow damasked walls, wishing she was as free as the bluebirds and butterflies perched on the vines drawn across the wall. Again, she wipes tears from her eyes, dries her hand on her dress, and turns from the crib.

Massa pulls the mattress off the wooden Dutch bed as he does most nights so Missus Lorelei can't hear the squeaking frame. He walks toward her, the stench of whiskey on his breath, and undoes her dress.

"Delphine!" Lorelei's voice resonates through the walls.

"Massa, please, Missus needs me," she whispers.

His eyes at her breast, drunk with lust, shine greedier than the infants in the crib for her milk. He places his finger in a hush at his lips, watching her pull the dress over her moist breasts and round belly.

"Delphine, come quick, gal!" yells Missus through several coughs in the master bedroom attached to the nursery where she sleeps. The one-year-old twins stir in the crib but don't wake. Massa Henry sneaks toward the window and out of view with his finger to his mouth.

Delphine unlocks and opens the door adjoined to Missus Lorelei's room. She finds her hanging half off the bed with a laudanum bottle in her hand. Thin blonde strands drape her face as she struggles to adjust her frame upright.

"Water," Missus says, her voice hoarse from coughs. She reaches for the jug on the far side of the nightstand.

"Don't strain yoself, Missus Lorelei." She rushes over, straightens her body on the mattress, and fluffs the pillows soured and damp from night sweats behind her back. Reddish-brown laudanum stains the top of her gown. "Let me do dat." Delphine takes the bottle from her hand. "Too much ain't safe, Missus."

"Just a drop this time." Her chest rattles with a deep cough as though her lungs heaved from her throat.

Delphine places a drop of tincture on her tongue to soothe her cough. Pouring water from the pitcher into the cup, she hands it to her, noticing Missus's sallow skin, purple-ringed eyelids, and sunken cheeks. The pinched mask of consumption she saw on old, deceased Massa. Missus Lorelei's poppa ran Magnolia with a kinder hand before he took sick and Missus married Massa Henry. Old Massa took ill and never seed daylight again, never leaving his bed.

Laudanum has become an addiction she fears will kill Missus before the illness. There's no stopping her from taking the only remedy from the painful coughing that started a month ago. Doc says she's getting better, but the coughs are worse. Delphine hoped in her weakened state she'd be more pleasant, but she's meaner than ever.

"How the twins? They keepin' you wake?"

"Dey be fine, though sleep fitful," Delphine states, taking the cup from her hand and placing it on the table.

"You must hate me, gal. To tend my sickness and my babies."

Delphine lowers her incensed gaze. *My babies* she wants to yell but dares not backtalk. Such words have only ever gotten her harsh words or a belt to her flesh. She winces at the pain she'd felt when Missus ordered slave hands to strip and whip her in the yard. For hours, she stood buck naked, her body raw, exposed to everyone, even her Maw.

She lifts her gaze, noticing the wretched look on Missus's face, sensing she's in one of her foul moods. For she only refers to the babies as her babies when she's angry.

Missus Lorelei tightens her eyes with subtlety. "The lawd will bless you, girl. You've done me such favors, given me babies my loins reject. I know how you think of me, taking your picaninnies as my own. But what good can you give them? I can afford them everything, a name, a station in life. Let me remind you not to speak a word of this to anyone. As far as the world's concerned, those babies sprang from my hips." She snorts a jab of meanness, pure vileness from her wicked throat, as though yellow-green slime poured from her mouth. "Thank heavens for your mixed breedin'. If they'd been born any darker, their fate might be different. I'd been told at the Forks of the Road auction you got some good genes. Yo Maw sired you from her old Massa. Good French blood I hear." Lorelei's chest heaves with a deep hack, rousing cries in the nursery.

Delphine starts toward the door.

Lorelei grabs her arm. "Come closer."

She steps toward the bed, tensing as Missus's hand rubs her pregnant belly as if it were her own. Her hands move to her leaking breasts as they have many times, caressing as if she were a blind woman seeking to discern their fullness. She stiffens as she squeezes and circles each breast as though it were a ripe fruit ready to eat. Sometimes she believes if Missus could claim her body as her own, she would, just for something real other than her dead womb.

"What's it like . . . the babies suckin' on your tits?"

Delphine's left eye twitches, resenting a word fit for a barn animal. Missus only uses it out of anger. She's in a dark mood, furious at the world for her ill health, a sickness that stole her looks. The fine features she took pride in are gone, leaving her raucous with hatred. She swallows her pride, realizing Missus Lorelei will never have a newborn's mouth nourish on her breast. Something she possesses they can't claim as their own. With spite she states, "Sumthin' good, Missus. Every woman shuld kno' nourishin' a babe. It's 'kin to a tingle, a warm liquid string drawin' relief through the nipple." At once, ashamed, she lowers her gaze and adds, "Sumtimes sore with constant nussin'."

Lorelei's nose flares as if detecting a foul odor. With a simper and wicked grin, she stares Delphine over for a long, silent moment with her shrewd eyes. "My lustful husband's gentler than the first time he had you, I hope?" she asks through another cough, squinting her eyes, expecting a reaction. When none comes, she sighs. "Oh lawd, gal, don't be coy. I gathered before I summoned you as my wet nurse that child yo Maw keeps is my husband's, kin to my unborn infant. Y'all part of Magnolia's family. I reckoned I'd get you 'way from the fields here with me. You should be grateful for plenty of food, clothes, a proper room, and my husband's pleasurin'." She tightens her eyes with a sly grin. "He satisfies yo needs now doesn't he, Delphine?"

She drops her chin, bracing for harsher words. It's no surprise Missus knows her firstborn belongs to Massa Henry. She looks just like the twins. Without a doubt, Missus heard Massa's groans and choppy breath in the nursery when he took her many nights on the mattress on the floor till she grew sore and his excitement ceased. She imagined her outside the door listening, boiling with anger that peaked to devil meanness. Missus's wise but feigns ignorance. Wavering without a response, she lowers her gaze, understanding Missus wants her to say yes. If she replies no, she'll appear ungrateful for the food, clothes, room, everything.

She lifts her gaze to Missus's artic-blue eyes, unable to answer a question she's often heard. Most evenings she burns with shame from the comfort she gets from Massa's touches. But those times come after Missus's nasty attacks and painful swelts, moments when Massa saw her with crocodile tears rolling off her chin and anger in her heart so tight she wanted to be incinerated by burning rage till her miserable life ended. His touch soothed her pain, made her flesh and blood with human needs. A woman again.

When Missus lost the third child, she started treating her nicer, praising her attractiveness, exotic mixed-breed looks, and firm body. She buttered her up with words thicker than curd, allowed her more rest and food she now realizes was nourishment for a healthy baby to come. She suspects Massa started visiting her bed at his wife's demand to fill her belly with a child. Missus knows no decency or jealousy just need for babies. Unknown to Missus, Massa's occasional trips to her bed grew into regular visits. He never stopped sneaking into her room, even while she was carrying twins.

"Does he pleasure you?" she asks again, catching Delphine's shamefaced expression. "I keep forgettin' you're just a child at fifteen. But there's no need for embarrassment now that you know men and conceived. You're a woman. And don't worry, I'm not offended by my husband's carnal desires. There's no lust for Henry. We tolerate each other in this matrimony of convenience devised by my deceased father. God bless his soul. Henry rose in station when he married into my family, one of the oldest families in Mississippi. I ask for only one thing from this dreadful marriage, children which I can't conceive."

Delphine bristles with disgust at being treated like a mare kept for breeding or as a cow pumped for milk. She tolerates the shame of giving pleasure to Massa Randolph. Pleasure Missus Lorelei's ailing body can't produce. The only good from this mess is a better fate for her children. Without flinching, she replies to a question she'd answered more than once before, wondering if she taunts her or the illness has addled her brain. Glaring at Missus with hateful eyes, she catches her tongue, holding back anger, but she can't control daggers in her tone. "No, Missus, no pleasure, just a woman's deed."

"Don't sass me with yo lies, Delphine."

Wails resound in the nursery, causing her milk to rise.

Missus circles the breast milk seeping through Delphine's dress with her finger. With a quick yank, she squeezes hard on her nipple. "Tell my husband, lyin' in your bed, not to disturb my children with his groanin'. Go now," she commands, releasing her painful pinch and turning away with a bloody hack.

INTO THE DEVIL'S ARMS

EARLIER, DELPHINE STOLE MISSUS'S BOTTLE OF LAUDANUM and placed several drops in Massa Henry's whiskey. The tincture always put Missus fast asleep, as it has Massa. His breath steadies, assuring Delphine a stampede of cattle couldn't rouse him from bed. She rises from the mattress as quiet as the moon creeping across the night, slips on her dress, slides shoes from beneath the bed like a knife through butter, and tiptoes toward the crib. Leaning over, she sniffs the twins' skin and cupid lips, still sweet with milk from feeding. Her chest aches, knowing she'll never hold them again or see their toothless grins and heartwarming giggles when she makes faces. Inches from snatching them up and fleeing, she stiffens and catches a tear rolling from her chin before it splashes the babies.

She rubs her eyes and stares over at sleeping Massa and the room she's spent two years nursing in. Two years Massa's woman. Two years wanting to escape through that dark, starry window just to catch a sliver of blue sky, bright sun, fresh air, and a whiff of the river's tangy breeze. A window she'd considered leaping from with the twins more than once. A sin the Lord may never forgive.

Can't take no moe of Missus's meanness and Massa's in-

satiable needs. Death looks better than days serving them. After long, too brittle-boned and dried up, she won't run. *No moe milk. No moe young flesh for Massa's seeds,* she thinks.

A sudden pang strikes her at the thought of leaving Massa. I *won't ail for him. It's wrong,* she scolds, rubbing her swollen belly. "Dat ain't no future foe bof us juz slo' death," she whispers to the unborn soul.

She'd carry the babies on her back if she weren't with another child, but their weight and a swelling belly is too much to haul miles north. Besides, she'd never forgive herself if something happened to them on the dangerous trails. Missus Lorelei's voice resounds honest in her thoughts. Loving the twins as she does, Delphine believes she'd give them a better life here at Magnolia.

"Youse my heart fo'ever, little ones," she whispers into their dewy faces with a soft kiss, pulling the cover over their legs. When a rising sob threatens to burst forth, she steps away from the crib, backing into the rocking horse with a gasp and a quick grasp, stilling the squeaky toy. Tiptoeing toward the door, she holds her breath and twists the clicking doorknob with a glance over her shoulder at Massa, peaceful in a whiskey-laudanum sleep. The door hinge whines a quarter-way open. Fearful of being caught, she squeezes through the narrow gap into the silent hall.

In the corridor, she pulls the door shut and doubles over between Missus Lorelei's door to evil and the nursery's door to pure goodness, wrapping her arms across her heaving chest, suppressing a sob. The invisible chains that bound her two years to Missus snap but refuse to free her from the twins. With one palm on the nursery doorframe and the other firmly on the doorknob, she breathes deep and tightens her grip on the knob.

Please, lawd, give me strength.

As though the spirits heard her prayer, a voice rises deep within her soul.

Go or youse will live yo dyin' days in dis place.

Now!

The urgent subliminal command rips her palm from the wooden doorframe. The entrance to a room she lost her youth and her babies. She glares at Missus's door and back at the nursery, the heart-rending sacrifice she leaves to the devils themselves. "God be with youse, little ones," she whispers. Turning away, she rushes along the hall, never looking back.

In the small garden behind Maw's cabin, Delphine appears a mad woman tear-stricken with rage for her plight as she pulls the handmade bag Maw sewed from an old blanket from beneath a row of turnips and checks inside for items she'd tucked away for several days. Cala and hot cakes. A jar of molasses. A sweetgrass basket filled with dried beef, cloth-bound cheese, nuts, seeds, and leftovers Maw pilfered from Massa's kitchen. A hand-sewn quilt. Extra clothing. The quarter eagle, and silverware she'd stolen from the cupboard. She figures Missus's expensive silver is worth more than the coin Massa gave her, money she needs up north.

Delphine wrinkles her nose when a caustic odor emanates from the bag. A small lumpy croaker sack Maw filled with several small satchels tied with flax cords contain liniments and salves made from various herbs, roots, and shrubs grown in her garden. A skill she learned from her mama and passed on to Delphine. Boneset and sage tonic for colds and fever. Rue for poison and plagues, although Maw warned her not to use it until the baby comes. An asafetida, turpentine, and garlic amulet to ward off disease. The healing burdock root and dogwood bark that cured many of Maw's pains. Castor oil fed to Delphine in teaspoons every night as a child. Comfrey oil used for rashes. And cocklebur roots and bluestone potion Maw explained stops the babies from coming when Massa has his way. Delphine used it many times, but the twins and the one she carries still came.

At the bottom of the pouch rest the twins and firstborn's braided locks, a good luck charm to keep dear to her heart. Maw feared she'd fetch attention on the roads and stashed slaves' clothes in the pack. She loops the traditional head wrap her people wear around the elegant chignon she'd worn in the main house, securing the ends with a knot, tucking the edges. At once, she unties the hot cloth from her head, unaccustomed to her curls being hidden.

"No. I ain't coverin' my head," she chides, placing it back in the bag.

A fit of anger and disgust overcomes her as she discards Missus Lorelei's expensive hand-me-down silk-calico dress, ripping and tossing it with the fancy shoes into a row of corn.

"I's free to dress and do as I's want. No moe Missus and Massa's need of my flesh. No bind to others' needs, juz my own." She inhales and exhales like a newborn, taking life's first breath, staring at the bright moon shining only for her. Baptized anew in its glow, Massa and Missus wickedness sloughs like white, viscous birth matter from her soul.

Moonglow brightens the dark, humid night as she undresses and withdraws the homespun clothes Maw weaved with her own hands from hemp. A linen petticoat. A brown skirt. Gray waistcoat. Plain but sturdy leather boots. Now she looks like a simple slave girl, not a well-kept Missus.

Slinging the sack over her shoulder, she turns around and gasps at two figures drifting toward the garden.

"Shush, chi_d . . . It's me. Youse late. I thought Massa done caught and chained ya to da bed like Missus done b'foe."

"Massa sho'd too early. I's drugged his whiskey with laudanum and snuck out while he slept," Delphine explains, staring at the familiar man beside Maw.

"Benoit wus bout to climb da nursery window a moment ago."

"I wus till Maw stopped me," Benoit says, stepping toward her.

"Ben? What youse doing here?" She hasn't seen her twin brother since Massa took her as Missus's wet nurse. Since Benoit was a kid, he's toiled the fields from sunup to sundown. Massa worked him to the bone and kept him away from his blood in another cabin.

"Takin' my sis way from dis place."

Ben's words soothe like sweet molasses glazing her tongue on a warm summer morn. A sensation only his voice affects, and she hasn't felt since Massa separated them. A comfort his presence always creates. Delphine steps toward a hardened man of fifteen, no longer the rail-thin boy known to her two years ago. His skin and hair reddish-brown from hours in the sun. She gazes up his tall frame at his changed face, etched with a world of pain, and runs her finger across a raised line running from his cheek to his jawbone. A deep lash he received protecting her from Missus's whip, a lash that clipped his face as he'd jumped in front of her. A deep gash opened his beautiful cheek and jaw. A long-healed wound, now a rooted scar. Delphine drops her gaze, afraid he will see what's become of her. She ain't that pure girl he once knew.

"Delphie, don't hide yo shame from me. Youse still my sis and nothin' change dat, not even Massa's sinful ways," he says, lifting her chin with his fist.

Ben's eyes hold nothing but brotherly affection, seeing her always as that sweet, untainted girl, but his assurances won't rid her of the awful things they'd done to her. She lifts her gaze to his beautiful, thick-lashed brown eyes like her own. "Youse a sight foe soe eyes. I's thought youse gone foe good."

He grabs her shoulder, crushes her into his chest, then releases her slowly. "I's never left. Massa done kept us apart, but youse always here," he says, patting his chest, "in my heart fo'ever, Delphie."

Delphine tries to speak, but emotions choke her words.

"Yo brother gone join the Union Army's colored regiment. When Maw told me what youse up to, I's figure I's help my sis to Union lines. Deys got camps to stay hidden from Massa tils da baby comes and youse ready to travel north."

"Lawd, boy, youse goin' get yoself killed," Delphine screeches, horrified. Ben's always been a fighter, and no words will talk him out of joining the Union. "B'foe my eyes I sees a grown man, but youse too young to fight a war."

"Ain't got no birth papers to say otherwise, b'sides I's fight wounded and bleedin' to death foe our people."

"Y'all ain't got time to chat. Best hurry, b'foe Massa and Missus Lorelei finds Delphine missin'," Maw says, pushing both behind the cabin toward a tree-covered path spangled with fireflies.

"I's can't leave foe sayin' bye to baby girl."

"Delphie, it'll rip yo heart out. Go while youse can."

"Juz a peek, Maw."

Delphine rushes toward the cabin, creeps onto the porch, and peers through the door at her sleeping, two-year-old girl curled on her side in the same bed she came into this world in. She scowls at the grayed, rough cotton blanket and the thin ticking mattress stuffed with corn shucks atop the wooden puncheon planks bored into the wall. She wishes her girl could sleep on the elegant white-lace-canopy crib's soft bedding with the twins. She steps inside with a burning urge to seize her from this god-awful place, but a realization halts her next step. She can't take her from Maw. Her firstborn's grown attached to her. She's Maw's now. Delphine's hands itch to touch and hold her one last time, but knowing she may never see her again is too painful.

She steps off the spick-and-span planks Maw always sweeps. "Cleanliness is godliness," she'd said with a scowl one day while fixing Delphine's messy bed. Maw made the modest cabin livable, homely with a constant, warm fire, sweet herbal scents, tasty meals, hand-stitched bedding with colorful patterns, and jars filled with blossoms from her garden. But the rickety one-room shanty will never match the luxury of the big house she admires.

Delphine steps backward with fingers to her puckered lips, peers through the closing door at her firstborn until the door closes, and then places a farewell kiss on the doorframe with her fingers. Gripping her chest, she slinks off the porch and around the side of the cabin toward Maw and Benoit, who are staring with worry etched across their wrinkled brows.

"Gods gone punish me foe leavin' y'all. Maw, please come with us."

"Child, there's nothin' out there foe me. Dis where I's b'long. B'sides, I's look after the chillun." Maw draws her brows and stares hard, brushing tears from Delphine's cheek. "Yo babies safe here with me." She caresses Delphine's belly with an anguished sigh. "Infant's ripenin' will make da journey difficult. Youse strong enough?"

"I'm leavin'!" she blurts with staunch defiance meant for her captors not Maw, then lowers her voice, staring at Maw with resentful eyes. "Dey can't have dis one. Dis my baby. I pray God bless my soul with courage to carry us bof."

Maw sighs, staring at Delphine's growing belly.

"Youse always been headstrong from da day youse came from my womb kickin' and hollerin' louder than yo twin brother foe da whole world to hear." She stares at Ben and Delphine, clasps her chest with a pained face, and catches her breath. Her lips tighten, but it does nothing to restrain emotions in her trembling chin and watery eyes. "It won't be easy. But I's pray every night and day youse find goodness in dis world. Ben, get my daughter and grandchild to safety and stay alive fightin' foe us," she says, grabbing them both in a firm hug.

Delphine fastens her arms around her and whispers, "Don't let da chillun fo'get me."

"Deys our blood and I's speak of youse till my blood runs cold. Dey goin' know 'bout deys mamma, Delphie," she whispers with an assuring squeeze. "Be safe and brave, my chillun," she says, then shoves them from her bosom, wiping her face. "Go on now, b'foe Massa comes lookin'," she demands, tears glazing her eyes in the dark.

"I's be back, Maw," Benoit says, pulling Delphine toward the shadowy trail behind the cabin.

Delphine snatches her hand from Ben's and turns around with a vision she'll never forget, a dreamlike image of Maw through a sparkle of fireflies vanishing through the trees toward the cabin. Before the big white house recedes in the distance, she gazes at the dark nursery window with a final goodbye to the twins, then turns and races onto the moonlit trail behind Ben. The last time Delphine crossed this path was her first day at Magnolia. A passage she'd spied freed slaves escape many nights through the nursery window.

The brackish river odor, humid air, and chirping critters enliven her senses as if she's seeing the world for the first time. A breeze brings a rush of liberation lost to Massa and Missus Lorelei. Her legs haven't moved this fast since Massa snatched her from the cabin at thirteen. The baby kicks in her belly as though delighting in the burst of speed. After mere minutes on the trail, her calves cramp and her breath becomes labored. Daily strolls around the home hadn't prepared her body for such exertion. She catches her breath and yells, "Ben, slo' down. My legs can't keep yo pace."

Benoit glances back, shaking his head. "Shush, Delphie. Deys hear us." He stops with his hands on his waist staring at his panting sister. "I's knows it. Youse been housebound too long. And with baby, yo body ain't ready foe dis. We's got miles before reachin' Union soldiers camped at da ole auction block. Now youse sho youse can do dis, Delphie?"

"I's fine, but can't keep up with yo horse legs," she says with a guffaw. The mention of Forks dampens the exhilaration. "Dat place scares me. Ain't nothin' good 'bout da Forks." The last time Delphine saw Forks of the Road, people gawked, poked, and inspected their flesh and teeth like prized cattle on the auction block. She teared up when Maw's clenched jaw strained her face as men patted her breast and behind in approval. The second day at the auction, Massa Henry and Missus Lorelei showed up and loaded them on a wagon headed straight to Magnolia Sunrise. She and Benoit were just seven and Maw twenty. Now, eight years later and freed slaves at fifteen, they're fleeing toward a place she'd left as an innocent child.

In eight years, she'd experienced things no child should know: men's lust, childbirth, evil in people's hearts, death, and pain and sorrow that plunged her to hellish depths she never wants to experience again. Mental and physical abuse has left her skin thicker than cow hide, her spirit disheartened, and her mind distrustful of others' intentions. Though flawed, she's much wiser.

Forty minutes later, the heavens conspire against their journey, dropping a downpour so thick it masks the pathway, dimpling the ground with puddles and mud covering her leather boots and dress hem. Rain pelts hard as nails, driving their clothes to their bodies in no time. Heaven's sudden angry tears pound the dusky trail, intensifying the worries in Delphine's mind. No rain in five days. Why now? It is as though the heavens deliberately forestalled their trek ahead. With that thought, lightning flashes and dances, ghosting the path and trees. Is the Lord warning them to go back or lighting their way in the dark? She chides her foolish, fearful mind, and races along the flickering path, searching for a tree to take cover.

A flash of lightning illuminates a tunnel beneath long fronds and overhanging Spanish moss atop a slight mound bordering the trail. They race toward the opening, scooting beneath dripping moss. Sheltered inside, they listen to the rain and occasional sloshing of feet, possibly of freed slaves or nasty paddy rollers searching for runaways.

"We's go when rain lets up," Benoit says, pushing his bag into the overgrown clay wall and resting against it.

Glad to rest for a moment but fearful of what else lies inside the loamy burrow, she peeps around the murky space for animals or someone else sheltering from the rain. When a rustle sounds at her rear, she slings a hard gaze toward the dark space for movement and gathers a tuft of moss from the floor, tossing it toward the area. Nothing stirs. Perhaps it was just fronds brushing the top of the burrow outside.

They are silent, only their breath resounding in the dark. Frogs croak nearby. Critters burrow in shrubs. Earthworms slither above ground. She and Benoit shelter among moss and vines, two of God's creatures trying to survive, just another test of their backbone. For a moment, she questions the toilsome journey. Will life be any better up north? Given what she's suffered, she can't believe she'd consider running back to Magnolia because of a minor inconvenience and discomfort.

Ain't nothin' worse than dat prison.

Taking the canteen from her waist and setting it on the mossy floor, she huddles into Ben's side, aching with leaking breasts and silent tears, worried the twins woke hungry for her milk, though they seldom do at night, only morn. She shivers, folding into the sodden dress, squeezing moisture and pain away, not bothering to wipe tears mirroring raindrops quivering puddles on the trail. A passage that leads to new beginnings. A better future for her unborn child.

Be brave foe da unborn one.

An hour later, rain ceases as fast as it began. The moon moves past clouds, gleaming through overhanging moss, awaking Delphine to a weighty mass gliding across her belly. Every muscle in her body tenses as she lifts her head and holds her breath, eyes widening on an enormous, glistening snake. Her pulse races and goose-flesh pimples her skin; she fears the reptile senses the baby in her womb and the child will move as it had earlier. A silent sigh of relief escapes her as it wriggles beneath her midriff to her thighs and coils along her calf, clinging to her leg as if it were a branch. She scrunches her face and tightens her lips, repressing an urge to kick it off, knowing it might incite the creature.

Horses and men's voices sound nearby. Ben springs up at the sight of the snake and turns his gaze to Delphine's frightened, wide-eyed gape. Afraid she'll scream and alert the approaching men to their hiding place, he cups her mouth tightly.

"With the rain and Delphine's condition, they couldn't have gotten far."

At the sound of Massa Henry's voice, a gasp rises in

Delphine's throat, muted by Ben's hand. Fear of Massa's nearness and the snake squeezing her leg, triggers sweat from her forehead to her brow. Every muscle constricts in her body except the wild animal beating in her chest.

"You sure that gal headed this direction?"

Delphine recognizes the voice of the nasty paddy roller she'd seen dragging runaways back to the plantation so often. Massa never joins the party of men. *He must be hotter than hell*, she thinks.

With the pound and splatter of horse hooves and men's voices, the snake tightens further, cutting off blood to her numbing foot and leaving it tingling with pins and needles. Delphine fears the serpent will snap back with a poisonous bite if the mares sense its presence and whinny loudly or stomp their hooves.

"Josie moe stubborn than a mule. I couldn't beat a word out of her. Even if I'd lashed her to a bloody pulp, she won't betray her children. She didn't have to say a word. Two sets of footprints behind her cabin leading to this trail I'm sure belong to Delphine and Ben. Let's keep on, they can't be far," Massa Henry says.

Delphine furrows her brows as her eyes well with tears, remorseful they've caused Maw a severe lashing. She swings her gaze to Ben's blazing glare and clenched jaw, sensing his muscles tense and chest constrict when Massa mentions beating Maw.

The horses trot past their hideaway, continuing along the muddy path. The snake loosens its clutch, unwinds, and glides to the side of the tunnel.

Delphine plucks Ben's sweaty hand from her mouth, releases a long-held breath, and yelps, "Snake, monster, bastard!" Words she'd wanted to scream the moment she first felt the slithering snake, now a fading vestige as blood rushes into her toes, and when Massa spoke of whipping Maw to a bloody pulp. Jolting upright, her head bumps the top of the burrow with a tumble of dirt and debris falling around her. With frenzied hands, she swipes at her hair and skirt, shuddering. "It wus on my belly."

Ben covers her mouth again. "Youse too loud, Delphie. We's gotta go before deys find us."

Delphine peeks her head through the fronds, inspects the trail, then scoots from the tunnel when it's safe. She steps back with her eyes on the spot the serpent slithered, afraid it's still there.

Ben slides from the opening, wiping fallen debris from his face and damp, wrinkled clothes. "It's moe likely a harmless garter snake," he says, laughing just as he'd done when a turtle snapped at her finger at six years old.

"It ain't no garter snake. Dat thang long as yo body," Delphine barks, still feeling the snake's wriggle on her belly and recalling how something had rustled when they entered the burrow. "It wus inside da whole time. It could've wrapped 'bout our necks and choked us in sleep," she says, shivering again at the thought.

"Longs it didn't bite, youse be fine," he says, dragging the bags from the tunnel. "We's got bigger worries than dat snake."

"Maw . . ."

"She's strong, Delphie. B'sides, Massa cares an awful lot foe Maw. He gave her a light whippin', nothin' moe."

Ben's right. Massa cares for them both. She'd seen it in his eyes more than once, it was as though his heart burst when he inflicted pain at Missus's command. Maw's safe as long as he's Massa of Magnolia. With a darting gaze around the black space, she reckons the twins woke hungry for her milk, alerting Massa and Missus to her absence.

When a rumble and voices sound behind the tunnel, Delphine glances around, expecting Massa to appear any minute atop the speeding steed, bind her wrist to the horse, and drag her back to Missus Lorelei's biting whip. Missus will lock her in the nursery and throw away the key for good if she's caught.

"Ben, we's gotta move."

"Youse read my mind, sis."

~

Feet slosh through puddles and wagons roll and rumble past the tunnel on a parallel footpath, the noise Delphine heard a moment ago. She and Ben peek through the trees, spying a small caravan of three horse-drawn wagons with families and a straggle of freedmen, women and children tramping alongside and behind the wearied convoy.

"Deys been leavin' plantations foe days, toward Union lines," Benoit says.

"Deys goin' to da same place, then we's join 'em. Massa finds us easier alone than with des people," Delphine says, grabbing Ben's hand with a sharp turn, ducking and weaving through the dark underbrush, fighting snapping branches and thick vines as her boots sink into swampy ground. She glances over her shoulder at Ben's irked scowl as he stumbles on vines. "Come on," she urges.

Delphine emerges through the thicket, gazing at bedraggled men, women, and children moving at a snail's pace, some in bare feet, others in shoes threadbare from miles of walking from distant plantations, determined to reach Union lines as she and Ben.

A haggard mother with a child in a sling on her back and meager belongings on her shoulder sways when her knees buckle beneath her dingy skirt. She shifts the child's weight, dragging her bare feet along the muddy path. In the moonlight, exhaustion hangs off the mother and child's faces, aching Delphine's heart and reminding her of the twins she, unlike the other mother, hadn't had the courage to bring. Why hadn't they tried? Benoit hauled sacks of cotton every day and could easily have carried her babies. But it's too late. They can't turn back. As though the woman heard Delphine's thoughts, she turns a crestfallen gaze to Delphine's face, then her belly, smiling and then looking away with the obedient timidness of slaves. Concerned for the woman and child, Delphine rushes toward the convoy.

"Delphie, stop!" Ben screeches, yanking on her waistcoat.

The driver of the wagon turns his head and tips his hat from his forehead, eying them for a suspicious moment. "If headin' to Union lines, y'all moe than welcome to join us."

"Yessa, dats where my sis and I's headin'," Benoit says.

"Alright then," the driver says, turning his gaze ahead.

Delphine scuttles beside the woman with the child in the sling. The girl lifts her head and coughs several times with a weak whimper. Her runny eyes glisten in the dim light as she extends her small arm. Delphine takes the girl's outstretched hand, hot as though warmed over a blazing fire, noticing a reddish rash on her face and arms. The mother, absorbed in the wagon ahead, doesn't notice Delphine run her hand across the child's forehead.

She's burnin' up.

When the woman's profile comes into view, Delphine sees the same rash runs along her neck and collarbone. At once, Delphine recalls the measles and rubella that spread through the slaves' quarters several years ago and worries the woman and child's illness is infectious. Before she can step away, the woman's knees give way. The child scowls and whimpers with the sudden dip.

"Ben, help me," Delphine calls, gripping and

boosting the woman's arm over her shoulder. The woman shivers with fever through her damp clothes. "Youse need to rest."

"Not till we's get to Union line. Soldiers give us medicine and shelter."

The woman's determination even in illness amazes Delphine. It ain't right she's on her feet while the buggy ahead has space for more people.

"Ben, take her arm."

Ben grasps the woman, flinging her arm over his shoulder as Delphine hurries toward the wagon driver who'd greeted them moments ago.

"Mista, please stop."

"Name's Joe," he says, swiveling his head toward Delphine.

She points toward the woman and child. "Deys sick and can't walk. Da wagon got plenty room to carry 'em."

With a hawk-eyed gaze, he peers at the woman and child and the others' judging eyes and brings the trotting horse to a halt. "Make room," he says to two women and a boy behind him. The boy drags a burlap sack to his side and pats the floor.

The older woman looks up at Joe with a scowl. "No, Joe. Youse don't know wat sickness deys carry."

"Scoot over, Sissy. Don't be heartless."

The woman pushes a spinning wheel into the corner and moves over, pulling a girl about Delphine's age into her side in alarm.

Ben hustles the woman and child toward the rear of the rickety buggy that plantations use to haul crops and hay, hoisting them between two stuffed sacks and a small trunk, wondering what it holds.

"God bless y'all," says the woman to Delphine and Ben with a feeble smile. The buggy rocks and rolls forward.

"Dat big ole heart goin' cause a world of trouble one day," Ben says, edging beside Delphine.

"I's juz like my brother."

The buggy stops again. The driver turns and lifts his black derby, wiping sweat from his shiny face. "Wat y'all waitin' foe," he says, motioning them aboard with his hand.

Racing forward, Ben hoist Delphine up and pulls himself aboard, sitting in front of the woman and sleeping child.

"The lawd looks after y'all like youse foe me," says the woman.

Delphine smiles but worries like Sissy that the illness may infect everyone, even her unborn child.

"I's Anabelle, and dis my girl, Georgia, short for Georgina."

"Dat's a beautiful name. I's Delphine and dis my brother Benoit." At once, remembering Maw's herbs, Delphine opens the bag, removes and unwraps two hotcakes, placing a scoop of comfrey and boneset in each linen rag. "Maw swoe by comfrey and boneset. Da herbs cure y'all's ails."

The woman takes the potion from Delphine's extended hand with a gracious nod. "A kind soul foe a beautiful woman . . . God bless youse with an angel. Anabelle's gaze slips to Delphine's belly. When's the baby come?"

Delphine recalls the brisk March night Massa released her and rolled on his back. At the moment his seed took root, she knew he'd put another child in her belly. She didn't need Missus Lorelei's doctor poking around to tell her when the baby would come. She learned from two births and from Massa Henry how to count five months. "I's havin' a December baby."

"I's pray foe da child," Anabelle says with a weak grin. Overcome with fatigue, she curls to her side, leans into sleeping Georgia, and closes her eyes.

Delphine catches the baby-faced teenage boy and watchful girl's curious stares in the wagon's front and smiles.

The boy's face broadens with a smile. "Names' Willy, and dis my sis, Beth."

"Dat my boy and girl, and wife, Sissy," Joe explains.

Delphine nods at the three, noticing Joe's russet, reddish-brown hues in the girl, which contrasts with Willy's light yellow-brown skin, acquired from his fawn-skinned mother.

Aware of everything around her, Beth turns her owl-eyed gaze at Simone, her lips narrow into a timid smile. With uneasiness in the corner, Sissy shifts her glare from Anabelle and Georgia, nods at Simone and Ben, and swings a squint back at Anabella.

"Where y'all come from?" Delphine asks.

"Lansdowne."

"Grants here in Natchez lookin' for colored soldiers. I aim to join 'em," Willy divulges.

"Dat's where I's headin'," Ben says with enthusiasm.

Joe twists his head around, hissing air through his teeth. "Boy, dey ain't puttin' guns in no black man's hand. Y'all end up doin' labor as teamsters, cookin' and cleanin' soldier's mess. And I's heard boys too young to fight ain't nothin' but gophers for higher officers. Y'alls work for yo clothes, food, and shelter, and no moe," he says, hissing through his teeth again. "Union camps no place to stay, juz shelter, a bed, and food foe movin' north."

"Not no moe. Back at the plantation, words got 'round dat General Grant set up camp at Rosalie Plantation. He's formin' a colored regiment to fight," Ben says.

"Pfft . . . I's believe it when I see it with my own eyes," Joe says.

Delphine listens as they babble on about the war, Lincoln's emancipation, and fighting for their people. With images of a blue-uniformed Ben dying bloody on the battleground, she wants to knock sense into his skull. She turns out the conversation and glances toward exhausted people trudging behind the wagon, struck immediately with a guilty conscience, wishing she could ease their suffering. But she can't help everyone. Dismissing guilt and disquiet, she rests her head on Ben's shoulder, gazing at the dark sky and the moon moving through the trees. She relishes the smell of petrichor rising from the dusky trail, the muggy breeze on her face, and her newfound freedom, but wishes her firstborn and twins were beside her. The sound of voices on another path dashes momentary elation, and she fears Massa's nearness and his men halting her journey.

A flutter spreads across Delphine's abdomen as they arrive at the Union soldier's outpost, a white canvas city along the dark grounds where Fork's trading block stood, now demolished. The quickening comes sooner than the other pregnancies. She supposes the rickety wagon brought on the fetal movement and being near the razed slave auction. Or is it fear of being captured? She dismisses her worries and soothes the twitching child with a rub of her belly, never voicing concern to Benoit.

Lanterns hang from trees and firelight illuminates the night as listless guards watch their arrival. The caravan slows to a stop behind a long train of freed slaves. More men, women, and children flood the town in waves. Voices resonate ahead. Delphine sits straight, taking in the makeshift porches made from carved wooden posts and poles with twig-and-branch roofs attached to many tents. Tree trunks, gathered from adjacent woods, line the center of the camp in large stacks. Wounded soldiers with bandages, absorbed in a card game, imbibe from tin cups around a table bordering a large A-shaped tent.

A man's voice commands ahead, stopping the slow-moving caravan. For an hour or more, they inched toward the commanding officer and several other soldiers, documenting every person's name, the plantation they'd left, and their master's name. A forceful voice booms, "Picket Anders and Jones."

Two colored soldiers appear, searching the possessions of the new arrivals. A commotion sounds when they remove furniture from a family's wagon and untie two mules and a horse they'd brought with them.

"Please, sah, dose my family's. It's alls we's got."

"Under the Confiscation Act, the Union may seize any property that belongs to your master and turn it over to the quartermaster," the officer in charge answers, while picket soldiers haul their items and livestock away.

Joe peeks around at Sissy with worry.

Delphine glances around the wagon at the sacks and the trunk, understanding Joe's alarm as soldier's approach the wagon. Sliding her hand inside her bag, she removes the quarter eagle and Missus Lorelei's silverware, sitting on the coin and stashing the silverware between her back and the cart wall.

"Names, plantation, owner?" the soldier in charge asks as he did with the others. Joe replies, "Dis my family," giving his wife and children's names, plantation, and master in a steady voice.

"You two?" the soldier asks, ambling behind the wagon.

"Ben and dis my sis, Delphine. We's from Magnolia Sunrise, owned by Massa Henry Randolph."

Delphine stares at Ben alarmed, wondering why they need their owner's name, fearing they'll send them back or alert Massa Henry to their whereabouts.

One soldier studies Joe's worn-out horse, deeming it

too old for the Union, while two colored soldiers drag the trunk and sacks from the wagon. Burlaps contain beans, flour, corn, flax, and cotton Joe brought from his plantation. Inside the trunk lay clothing, bedding, and a jiggling pouch.

"Dat money's mine. I's work hard foe it. Massa and I's had an arrangement. He's paid me foe my work," Joe says, growing angry.

"It belongs to the quartermaster now."

They return the trunk back to the wagon, keeping the burlap sacks and money.

Sissy grips Joe's arm as he rises with anger, pulling him back onto the seat. "Let it be, Joe."

Tight-lipped, hands fisted, Joe stares at his wife, mumbling, "Dat's our security north, Siss."

The soldier steps toward the spinning wheel. "Please, my mama left me dat," Sissy pleads.

"You a seamstress?"

"Yassa. I's make and mend clothes."

"You'll will come in handy here," he says, stepping off the wagon.

"What you got in the satchel?" the soldier asks Delphine.

"Juz food and medicine foe my baby, sah," she says, rubbing her belly.

"When's the child due," he asks, searching through her bag.

"December, sah."

His dark-eyed gaze travels from her face to her breast and belly with an expression she'd seen in Massa Henry's hungry eyes. She frowns and wraps her arms around her belly, lowering her gaze to the soldier's hands, which search her and Benoit's bags but find nothing for the quartermaster.

Delphine's thankful the coin and silverware weren't discovered, but suppresses her relief, mindful of Joe's misfortune.

The soldier shakes Anabelle and the child with no response.

"Deys tired, sah. Been on deys feet foe hours. Names Anabelle and Georgia, from my plantation," Joe lies.

The soldier drops his head, studying the sleeping child lying face down on the wagon, her face obscured in her mother's side. Anabelle opens her eyes. Startled, she sits upright, inching away from the man like a frightened child, lifting her collar to her chin as though in modesty.

Delphine has seen that look before. She imagines it is the same expression she herself wore when Massa trapped her in the garden. Someone's hurt Anabelle too. Or she woke from a frightful dream.

"I won't bite you, girl," the soldier says.

Delphine parts her lips, ready to tell the soldier the child's sick, then stops, catching Anabelle's slight head-shake. Anabelle doesn't ask for medical aid even though the child burns with fever and needs immediate help. Delphine frowns, perceiving there's a reason she's afraid and silent. Given Sissy's fear of contagion, she's surprised she hasn't screamed out to the soldier that they are diseased. With the same worried expression, Sissy sits tight-lipped in the corner. Her behavior reminds Delphine of the many times slaves on the plantation protected each other whenever one committed a misdeed.

The soldier scribbles something on his pad, pauses a moment gazing at Anabelle and the child as though a flitting thought were crossing his mind, then proceeds to the next wagon.

~

Several hours later, soldiers guide the caravan away from the encampment, circling the caravan back in the direction they came. The soldiers keep many of the freedmen, leading them inside the camp and away from their families.

"Why's we's turnin'? We's can't go back dat way." She yanks her bag from the floor, tugging on Ben's arm. "Let's get off now."

Ben grasps Delphine's arm and leans over the side, looking ahead at the curving convoy. "Wat's happenin', Joe?"

"Y'all settle down. Deys takin' us to another Union camp."

"We's be fine, Delphie," Ben says, releasing her arm.

Ten minutes pass before the wagon heads west to a steep, terraced descent under the bluffs. The caravan inches alongside the wharf where steamers and flatboats unload cargo and passengers. In the gray light of twilight, Delphine recognizes the place where she arrived as a child with other slaves and the sharp ascent they marched toward Forks.

Deys takin' us 'cross da river, she thinks as the wagon winds near the waterfront past a cluster of shacks and a saloon, tavern, and trading post built on stilts. When the caravan moves from the water, moving west through a wooded trail, she grows anxious again. A sweet scent fills the air, emanating from a thicket of trees. Peach trees. But the branches are bare from harvest. The sugary essence emanates from fallen, rotting peach carcasses picked over by birds and other scavengers on the ground. Is this what Maw saw? As they crossed the river from ole Massa's plantation from Louisiana to Natchez, she'd overheard the slave trader speak of wild peach groves Indians planted under the bluff years ago before they were enslaved or run off their land.

Delphine's gaze climbs the steep semicircular bluff with an eerie chill coursing through her body. Quickly her eyes descend to the basin floor and toward the approaching wooden fence guarded by colored soldiers.

"We'll assign able-bodied men and women work as

long as you remain in the camp," a soldier yells. "Men report to this post for jobs in the mornin'."

"Claim yo Sibley," another soldier yells as they continue through the gate.

Delphine's brows arch. "Sibley?"

"Tents. I's overheard soldiers above say there ain't enough Sibley tents. Dats why dey kept men at da camp above."

"Ben, I didn't leave Magnolia to work foe Union soldiers."

"Deys pay, Delphie. We's earn money foe our work. With baby, work won't be hard labor."

"Any work is labor with child, Ben. And I ain't no cook, seamstress, or laundress. I ain't cleanin' no filthy clothes."

"Girl, youse won't survive a day a freed woman with dat thinkin'. Juz remember wat Massa done to yo body for two years. We's leavin' slavery behind and startin' a new life as free people, Delphie. It' won't be easy."

Delphine nods, knowing he's right. She's gotta fight for her people and her unborn child's freedom just as the soldiers do.

The wagon rolls inside an encampment much like the Union camp above the bluff. But the tents are larger and conical. A few slab shanties placed side by side in rows line the soggy grounds.

"Soldiers left des tents?"

"Or died," Ben adds.

"Dat ain't right, placin' us in dirty tents where wounded and ill soldiers died."

"Dirty, secondhand tents better than sleepin' outdoors," Ben scoffs, throwing her a sharp stare. "Youse spoiled in Massa's big house. Dat life long gone now."

Ben knows nothing of the abuse she lived daily, Missus Lorelei's bitter ways, or Massa's groping when she didn't want it. She deserved every ounce of pampering, but it didn't mend her pains.

Past the entrance, a dreary scene unfolds. "Ben, we's can't stay here." Delphine eyes what looks like a purgatory for lost souls not a passage of hope, a prison granting freedom only through life's ultimate escape, death. Magnolia's slave quarters' neatly lined cabins shaded under rows of live oaks and Spanish moss look like heaven compared to this place. Pots, kettles, crates, barrels, and clotheslines dangle beside uncomely tents. Lopsided chimneys beside makeshift shanties flank the main path that cuts through the center of the camp. On the outskirts, a trench surrounded by shovels and two carts sends a shiver down her spine.

She pinches her nose against the acrid stench of urine and human refuse emanating from muddy puddles beneath the wagon wheels which is made sharper by her heightened sense of smell. Human waste, charred food, faint smoke from shoddy chimneys, and the rot of disease and death she'd detected as a child when smallpox infested ole Massa's plantation across the river.

"Dis place ain't good, Ben."

"Dis temporay, Delphie, juz till youse have yo child . . ."

"Wat in God's name youse thinkin', Ben. I ain't havin' my child in dis place."

"Shush, Delphie. Youse loud as a horn."

Delphine pushes Ben away with a scowl and whips her head around to a disturbing scene of tired, sick, and injured people relieved to find refuge after a long journey from distant plantations. She catches sight of a man's tattered, blood-soaked sleeve and winces at the glistening bone-deep gash running from his forearm to his wrist. The ripped shirt reminds her of runaways returned to Magnolia, clothes bitten to shreds by slave patroller's tracking dogs.

She sighs in thought. *Freedmen marchin' to dey's final journey.*

But dis ain't her final stop.

She takes a deep breath and glances at Ben, hoping to persuade him one last time. "The baby ain't safe here with sick folks. We's in danger da longer we's stay. And only miles from Magnolia, Massa bound to come foe my baby. We's need to leave now." The unborn child kicks and flutters, sending a sharp pain from her belly to her hipbones. She sucks in a sharp breath to conceal pain from Ben but worries something's wrong with the unborn as she rubs the child twisting beneath her undulating belly.

"Delphie, stop whinin'. We's as needy as des folks. Got no way but our feet and no guide north. I's promised Maw to keep y'all safe and dis place safe from paddy rollers and Confederates till we's leave. B'sides, we get payin' Union jobs, money foe food, clothes, and a way north."

She stops nagging Ben. His instincts are always right. But her mind won't relinquish the grim image of the trench and shovels.

"We's stay with Joe and his family. Deys good folks," Ben says.

Joe brings the wagon to a stop in front of a wide tent, dismounts, and pats the tired horse. "I's find water for y'all and da animal," he says, wandering toward the main path and glancing around the camp.

Willy and Ben step off the wagon and inspect the tent. Delphine follows behind Sissy and Beth, leaving Anabelle asleep on the sack, wheezing troubled breaths next to the tranquil child.

She lifts her skirt and treks through deep muck inside the canvas where several women and children sprawl on makeshift beds built on wooden stilts a few inches above the damp earth floor. Underneath beds lie protective rubber sheets for their belongings. Embers in a small firepit peter out with a plume of smoke rising to the ventilation hole where a tripod keeps the tent upright. Ten empty beds circle the tent. Delphine wonders why they're unused. Did other people sleep there? Did they leave the camp or die?

"Beg pardon," Ben says, backing toward the entrance, bumping into Willy and Sissy. "We's thought dis tent empty."

A young woman, no more than nineteen, lifts her head from a rolled blanket used as a pillow and rubs her eyes, peering at the group. "Ain't no rules in dis place. Youse sleep wherever a bed is free. Youse welcome to dose," she says, pointing at the empty beds. "Others gone," she explains.

"Deys leave da camp?" Delphine asks.

The girl's face drops. "Not the way deys came." She turns and lies on the bed again.

Ben glances at Delphine's sour face. "We's stay here," he says.

"Dis our home foe now," Sissy says to Willy and Beth. Undoubtedly it would be their home for much longer than they'd planned, given their pilfered savings.

"It ain't no home, but it'll do till we make moe money," Willy says, stepping toward an unoccupied bed.

Delphine catches her breath when multiple pinpricking pains roll across her abdomen.

Sissy notices Delphine's wince and strolls toward her. "Youse in pain?"

"Juz da baby kickin'."

Sissy's eyes narrow. "I's a midwife on the plantation and knows pain when I's see it."

"Thought youse a seamstress."

"Dat a big old lie to save my mamma's spinnin' wheel from da quartermaster. It b'longs to my family. I's brought many babies in da world, not clothes," she says, placing a firm hand on Delphine's belly. The baby moves with her touch. "Heed dose pains."

Delphine nods and smiles. "I's will ma'am." She escapes Sissy's studious eyes and exits the tent, gazing above the circular bluff to the Union soldier's fort.

Why's da lawd bring us here? Dis ain't no place to be.

Regret grows with her hasty decision. Before running, she should have stayed at Magnolia till the baby came. The longer they stay in Natchez, the more likely that Massa would find them here. *He won't give up till he brings Missus Lorelei her baby, my baby.* By now she'd be miles away if they hadn't gotten on Joe's wagon. She sighs, glancing around the dismal grounds. Maybe Ben's right. *Dis place safe from paddy rollers foe a few days.*

More freed people arrive at the gate. Massa could charge through on his horse, searching every tent until he finds her. Will soldiers let him drag her back to Magnolia even though Lincoln freed them?

She gazes around the encampment for an escape, stopping at an opening in the fence beside a wide A-shaped tent. She breathes more calmly, noticing stars fading in the periwinkle sky, reminding her of the trip from Louisiana across the river on a flatboat with Maw and Ben. Another pain rolls across her abdomen.

Da lawd punishin' me foe leavin' my chillun. I's know it.

She breathes deeper, imagining rocking the twins in the nursery with bluebirds and butterflies on yellow walls until the pain subsides.

Flies rise above a fetid puddle like a cattle's hind. She gags and moves toward the wagon, catching Anabelle's blank gaze across the way staring at but not seeing her with reddish eyes worse than the night before. She slumps in slow motion beside the sleeping child, shutting her eyes.

~

Women and children emerge from tents, beginning morning rituals around smoky firepits. Steam rises from boiling kettles and cooked pork wafts from skillets, fusing with rancid smells over the grounds. Delphine's stomach growls. She retrieves her bag and unwraps Maw's hotcakes, glancing at Georgia and Anabelle, still asleep on the wagon, wondering when they last ate. *Deys be hungry when deys wake*, she thinks, placing two wrapped cakes by their sides. *Maw made moe than enough. Soldiers give 'em rations soon.*

Though hungry, the overpowering stench of human feces subdues her appetite. *Eat foe da little one.* She forces several bites, reaches for the canteen at her waist, then realizes it's gone. It's not in the wagon or her bags. *Da burrow.* She'd removed it from her waist and placed it by her side. In her alarm over the snake, she'd left it inside the mossy tunnel. The horse laps at a pail of water Joe collected moments ago, making her thirstier. Ahead, a woman empties water from a pail into a wide barrel under a wall-less shed with a sloping roof. Delphine trudges across the swampy grounds, pausing under the shed. "Is dis water foe da camp?"

"Yes, foe everybody."

"Where's it come from?"

"Yonda, from da creek," she says, gazing beyond the barricade toward the underbrush. "It's our drinkin', cookin' and washin' water" she explains, lifting the empty pail.

Delphine dips the scoop, swallowing several gulps. Wiping water from her mouth, she glances around the camp full of women and children, noticing only a handful of men. "Where all da men?"

The woman lifts her gaze toward the bluff. "My paw and brothers work above foe soldiers. Dey keep men separate from women and chillun, except ole and sick men," she says with a stricken expression as a crippled man hobbles toward them.

A woman's frightful screech pulls Delphine's attention toward the wagon.

Anabelle.

She races toward the wagon, slowing when Sissy and Beth exit the tent with frightened faces, and then stares at Anabelle slumped over on her knees, her sobs that of a wounded animal. A scene she'd seen often in the slave's quarters, the wail of loss, pain, and rage.

"We's goin' die! Deys cursed us with disease. Joe, I's told youse b'foe deys got on da wagon!"

"Mama, stop," Beth says, pulling Sissy away from the wagon.

Delphine perceives Anabelle's agony, clutching her heart as she reaches the rear of the cart. "No, lawd," she pleads under her breath.

Splayed on her back, the child stares at the sky, unblinking. A place her eyes no longer perceive. Unconcerned for her safety, Delphine pulls herself onto the cart and drops to her knees, wanting to comfort Anabelle, but there's no consoling a mother who's lost a child.

Georgia's outstretched arm, hot with fever hours ago, extends from Anabelle's waist, cool to the touch. Her soul departed while she lie motionless on the wagon floor without a sound or whimper of pain. Has she been dead since they boarded the caravan?

Anabelle's sobs shift to a fit of coughing, contagious hacks like those she'd heard many nights coming from Missus Lorelei. She coughs again, splattering Delphine's hand and Georgia's dingy gray dress with crimson specks.

Alarmed, Ben races toward the wagon, notices the child, and yells toward the camp, "We's need a docta!"

Anabelle collapses on top of Georgia, refusing to leave her side.

"We's need a docta," Ben screams again.

"Dey ain't no docta here, juz Miss May. She's a nuss," the limping man Delphine had seen moments ago replies, pointing at the large A-shaped tent near the abandoned wooden barracks. "Doctas don't come down here. Dey only above at Fort McPherson."

"Y'all get off," Joe says to everyone. "Dat tents too far to carry 'em. I's take 'em in da buggy." He hops aboard and steers the wagon toward the medical tent.

Anabelle's crouched figure bounces with the child in her arms as the wagon speeds away. Death was in the girl's runny eyes when Delphine approached her on the trail. Was she reaching out for help when she raised her fevered arm? She'd smiled like an angel ready to leave this world. In a matter of hours, she's gone. Delphine rushes into Ben's chest, drops her head, and weeps. "Why da lawd takes dat poe child? It ain't right."

"She's betta off in his hands, not dis cruel world."

She was right to leave the twins. It's too dangerous for children. Her eyes catch sight of the trench again. A place of death.

"We's won't be here long, Delphie."

Ben was wrong. Days turned into weeks, and weeks into months. Three weeks after arriving, Beth and George contracted the smallpox that had riddled the camp. They hadn't known the tent carried disease. First the women and children they shared the tent with passed, then Beth and George. Like Anabelle and Georgina, they rest in a mass grave beneath a peach grove. Sissy took to bed for days, refusing food and water. Delphine stayed by her side, forcing water into her mouth, assuring her Beth and George were in a better place. She pressed that her only son needed her to live. But she doesn't know if he's still alive. Sometimes, she believes Sissy wishes to die in this place with her husband and daughter. Willy keeps her earthbound in this place though he hasn't returned in weeks.

Too young to fight, Willy was assigned to be a Union

scout, alerting Union soldiers of Confederate movement in the surrounding areas. Once or twice, he'd escaped to visit his mother with a few rations. The last time, he informed Delphine of Ben's recruitment into Grant's colored regiment.

"Ben's a soldier now."

Asleep the morning he left on assignment with Willy, she hadn't had a chance to say goodbye. "He got his wish," Delphine replied, saddened and feeling abandoned.

A month has passed since Willy's last visit. Now it's she and Sissy grieving their losses together in a place that brings no solace, just a struggle to stay alive. Assigned jobs as laundresses in Sud's Row, work became a respite from their worries. The money promised to them as laundresses hasn't touched their lye-cracked hands; however, the disagreeable laundering continues. Soaking. Scrubbing. Rinsing. Wringing. Boiling lice and infection from clothing and bedding. Bluing yellowed clothes white. Ironing and starching. The ritual keeps her mind off Massa capturing her. But after three months, she's sure he's stopped searching. Days when she's confronted with bloodied and bullet-riddled uniforms, her fear for Ben intensifies and she imagines a gunshot to his head or heart. An instant death. To vanquish the thought, she'd scrub the blood so hard her hands would blister and ache the next morning. But as December grows closer, another concern rises, giving birth to her child in this hell.

People crowd the encampment in numbers for sanctuary. Security Delphine hasn't found just misery. At moments, she longs for the twins, the yellow nursery, and Magnolia's luxuries, but she can never go back. Here, the only consolation she's gained is inspiration from wandering missionaries. After mindless hours of laundering, she pines for Sunday Bible studies. To her surprise and heartache, one Sunday, she'd wandered into the empty barracks and found an abandoned Bible beside a blank chalkboard. The missionary's abrupt departure left her with deeper sorrow.

A new purpose inspired Delphine to take up the Bible and continue the missionaries' cause. She offered illiterate women and children reading and writing studies from the Testament. With such despair surrounding the camp daily, learning offered hope. Her skills are rudimentary, but it's enough for those with none. Twice a week they gather in the wooden barracks, learning one Bible verse at a time. Though difficult to decipher, the words provoke discussion and consolation in a place of uncertainty.

November arrived with scant rations from Union soldiers, who are dying from starvation, smallpox, and dysentery from fetid water along with the others. With meager sustenance, soldiers forage the woodlands and loot many nearby plantations for food. Delphine and Sissy start eating one meal a day to stretch the small rations of flour, beans, potatoes, salt pork, and dried vegetables longer. After weeks of little food and diminished rations, Delphine worries Sissy's lost too much weight. Her clothes hang loose around her slim frame, and her collar and shoulder bones protrude from her top. Potatoes and hardtack—biscuit made of flour and water— are the only food to stave off hunger. The large jar of molasses Maw packed has dwindled to half a jar, as they used a smidgen to sweeten boiled water for tea and spread on hardtack. Their sole source of protein, salt beef, finished a week ago, leaves them always hungry for fat in their diets, as it does many in the camp.

Days when she wanders to the creek for water, she imagines the bare peach trees heavy with fruit and most nights dreams of gorging on the juicy flesh till her stomach bursts, waking with cramps from hunger pangs. A few months ago, she gathered a bucket of peach pits left by scavengers and cleaned, boiled, and baked them over fire as Maw showed her years ago. Maw drank peach pit tea to cure an upset stomach. But she and Sissy drink it to stave off hunger pains. At night, the peach and almond scent soothes them before bed.

Delphine believes they will die of despair before starvation, but evening mourning rituals give them hope in their darkest moments. Neither illness nor malnutrition stops the worshipful gathering of men and women, praying for the dead. A collective spiritual euphoria inspired by handclap-enlivened worship, song, and dance resounds throughout the night. The ritual feeds a need greater than food, freedom. Delphine and Sissy huddle together in prayer for Sissy's departed family, and Benoit and Willy's safe return. A few dawns, they woke with many in the barrack. Clustered in sleep. Drunk from rapture or delirium of hunger.

When the baby stopped kicking weeks ago, Delphine worried poor nourishment weakened the child as it has her. Just days from giving birth, she won't have the stamina to force a baby from her hips. No matter how often she protests, Sissy, skin-and-bones, continue to share her meals, eating half and leaving the rest for her. "Eat foe the little one. I's be fine till soldiers bring rations any day, now," she says with certainty every time.

Has hunger muddled her brain? Her biggest fear is Sissy will die before the newborn comes. "Siss quit being stubborn. The child and I's won't survive alone. Don't leave me."

"I ain't goin' nowhere."

"Youse my family now, Siss."

As she and Sissy grow thinner, listless, time slips past with silent dread, no reassurance from soldiers.

With two potatoes, a half sack of flour, and Maw's molasses dwindling, they won't make it much longer if food doesn't arrive. Delphine wonders if the Union cares. Have they abandoned them to die and rot in the camp?

∽

One of the bleakest Mississippi winters in years leaves everyone in the camp vulnerable, many dying from exposure in makeshift shelters with no access to coats, shoes, or extra blankets to keep warm. Western winds howl off the river and pound flimsy canvases, cutting a wintry blast through slits and cracks. White condensation rises from Delphine's trembling lips as she shivers in sweat-soaked clothing. Her water broke an hour ago, but feverish and weak, she couldn't move. But now, with a sharper pain, she throws the cover from her body, plucks the asafetida amulet from her collar, which does nothing for her suffering, and rolls in agony from the mat to the frigid earth floor. The frosty air soothes her hot skin and the rash coating her face and neck. A spasm, more painful than the last, rolls across her pelvis, prompting a guttural groan.

Her legs buckle as she struggles to stand, forcing her to her knees. She inches to the center of the tent, looking over at Sissy tucked beneath the blanket. "Siss . . . baby comin'. Sissy?" When she doesn't respond, Delphine crawls toward her, arched with pain, trailing blood behind her ragged dress tail.

"Sissy, it's time." Delphine shakes her waist, pausing in the eerie quiet. She lifts the blanket and rolls Sissy over with a sharp gasp. "Sissy? Siss? Sissssss! Please, wake up!" She drops her forehead to Sissy's chest. "Youse can't leave, not now." Delphine lifts her gaze to Sissy's serene expression, a peaceful image of sleep, but no breath flows through her body.

"Please, Lawd, please . . . Wake up, Sissy. You ain't leavin' me now, not now!" She rocks Sissy's waist and pumps her chest, trying to bring life into her stiff body. "Lawd, give her back! Wake up, Sissy! You promised!" She drops her head onto Sissy's silent chest that beat with life just hours ago. "Lawd, why? She's all I's got. I's can't do dis alone."

Delphine snivels and wipes a fallen tear from Sissy's wizened, ashen-brown cheek, rubbing her bluish finger-tips as though burnishing the skin with warmth. Sissy's flaky lips had frozen in a smile as though joy swelled her heart at death. A tie ripped open by the wind flaps back and forth, sweeping a frigid draft toward the makeshift bed and across Sissy's body. Exposure took her in her sleep. She hadn't died as she'd thought she might from smallpox, which claimed her husband and daughter. After several weeks of sparse food, starvation whittled her to bones, no fat to protect her from expo-sure. Delphine shivers, reaches over the mat, and catches the flapping canvas with a quick fastening of the burlap ties Sissy constructed a week ago.

"Ahh!" She slumps over her knees with an acute spasm. Another pain, too strong to tolerate, drops her unconscious to the floor. Five minutes later, she wakes with a feverish delirium obliterating what occurred be-fore she fainted. A sharp twinge warns the baby's com-ing. Delphine's mind sees an illusion of Sissy rising and sitting next to her, though her lifeless body remains on the bed.

"Delphie, don't be scared. Youse goin' have dis child now . . ." Sissy points at the center beam. *"Hold dat pole tight and squat. Baby falls quicker and easier."*

Delphine crawls across the freezing room, stops, and clutches her belly with a guttural groan. She continues toward the center of the tent, back arched to restrain the spasms. Lifting her skirt above her thighs, she grips the pole with simultaneous moans and cries.

"She's comin' fast, Siss."

Grunting and squeezing the wooden post, she pushes with a hellish scream, straining till her heart flutters and consciousness verges on faintness.

Delphine drops her head onto the pole, drawing quick breaths. "Lawd, give me strength." With a grunt, she arches her spine and thrusts her head back, pushing, shifting on her ankles, knees, and hips, burning from holding the squat. A searing pain tears through her birth canal.

"Ahhhhh! God help me, Sissy!" She pants, gripping the steady pole with another groan. "Siss, I can't do dis."

"You must and will, Delphie. Push, child."

In Delphine's illusory perception, Sissy rises like a current from the bed, kneeling beside her with a firm hand on her back, rubbing and bolstering her spine, but it's her own determination holding her upright.

With several pushes, the baby's head drops between her thighs. Her eyes fall to the double-wrapped umbilical cord around the infant's neck, alarmed.

"Child can't breathe!" she yells, panting and reaching for the infant's neck.

"Calm down and bring yo child into dis world."

Pushing harder and holding the child's slippery head with one hand, the infant's shoulders appear. Delphine wobbles back on one elbow with the imagined help of Sissy and pushes and pulls the newborn girl from her womb. But the infant's bluish hue sends fear through Delphine's mind.

"KNIFE!" she screams, glancing toward the other end of the tent, wondering why Sissy hasn't moved. "Please, Sissy, get da knife. Baby can't breathe."

"Bite it, Delphie. It's da only way. Now, child."

With no time to waste, Delphine lifts the child to her mouth, wraps her lips around the cord, and bites into the dense tissue, gnawing through gelatinous matter for several minutes, veins spurting blood over her face, neck, and chest and coursing along her arms. She swiftly untangles the umbilical and ties a knot as though someone's hands guide her action.

When the child doesn't cry, she raises her in the air. "Breathe, please breathe!" Recalling Maw's hard spank to her firstborn, she whacks the child across the bottom, rousing an infantile wail. She laughs, falling onto her back, the infant's warm body radiating steam in the chilly air.

"Siss, I's did it."

Cries, fits of laughter, love, and pain rack Delphine's body as she admires the child she holds aloft. She pulls the skirt hem up and over the child's body and scuttles off the icy floor toward the bed, swaddling the infant in the blanket. "Youse warm now, little Sissy." The spontaneous name appeared unplanned, prompting a glance toward Sissy beaming with joy.

Delphine shivers not from the frigid night but chills from a high fever. Her top hangs off her exposed, thin shoulders, wet with sweat, birth fluid, and blood. She musters strength, crawls to Beth's bed, and fetches the extra bedding Sissy refused to remove and forbade her to touch as if her departed daughter would return.

"Fo'give me . . ." She peers at Siss before taking the blankets from the mat. "Child's cold."

Sissy nods. *"Take it foe little Sissy. Youse done good, Delphine."* Her body appears to float to the matt; her eyes flutter closed with a bright smile. Delirium fades in a flash, showing Delphine the truth in Sissy's cadaver blue lips and pasty brown skin. But feverish and weakened, hallucinations trick her mind. One moment, Sissy lies lifeless on her back, and the next, life revives through her body as she shifts sideways, drawing the covers over her shoulder.

Afterbirth oozes down her thighs as she makes her way back to the newborn. Fearing the tiny, glistening girl will freeze to death, she removes and wraps her skirt around the squirming infant and peels the bloody, sweat-soaked shift from her body to the floor. Lying beside the child under the blankets, she pulls her into her hot chest, spotted with the reddish rash of smallpox. "Shush now, be warm till I's make a mornin' fire, little one," she whispers, folding her arms around the quivering infant. She remembers a lullaby Maw sang to her as a child, humming most of the song and whispering the last refrain.

> "Jes lay yo head upon my bres;
> An' res', an' res', an' res', an' res',
> My little colored chile . . ."

The temperature sinks lower in the night, too low for Delphine's thin body and weak heart. Hypothermia sets in as she drifts in dreams to the warm, bright-yellow nursery with little Sissy in her arms. She places her newborn girl in the crib beside the twins and strolls toward the window. Maw and Ben wave to her from the small garden behind the cabin as her heart gives a final flutter.

～

Winds subside at sunrise over a familiar wagon rolling to a stop. Colored auxiliary soldiers serving as stewards come for bodies death claimed in the night. One steward enters the tent, pausing at blood trailing from a covered figure to an uncovered woman who'd died with a smile. He crouches beside the mat, peels back the blanket, gasps, and glances away. Anger drives his fist into the muddy ground. The bloody mess around the wooden post reveals the girl gave birth in that spot alone, as the other woman's clothes are unsullied. He recalls the beautiful girl when she entered the camp glowing with child. A child that might have survived with warmth and medical care.

He turns his head around and winces at the girl's nude, gaunt figure. She'd removed the bloody shift and swaddled the baby in her skirt for extra warmth, exposing sharp shoulder blades, ribcage, and hipbones that protrude through her translucent skin. Bloodstains smear her lips, chin, neck, hand, and fingernails. In the center of the tent, he notices the curled umbilical cord on the floor and glances back at her face, realizing what she'd done. Incipient smallpox rashes her skin. In her weakened state, he perceives she'd spent every ounce of strength to deliver the child whose time was short before dying in the night.

He's seen horrific deaths in two months as a steward but never a newborn and mother entwined in a frozen embrace. He draws the blanket over their bodies with a silent prayer. Clearing his throat, he summons his voice. "Moe bodies here," he hollers to the other steward outside.

Two men bearing shovels stand over a deep trench heaped with bodies, unaware of the presence beside them. They begin a routine they've performed every day since the frigid winter arrived. Shoveling dirt over women, men, and children who, finding only death, faced their demise in a place of refuge.

When dirt covers the young woman and her infant, the unseen woman backs away, turning around, revealing Delphine in her pregnant form. She walks along the center of the camp, past the medical tent and large barracks where she taught and prayed, and past the many dying in their tents toward the exit.

"We's free now, little one."

She strolls toward the exit she'd yearned to flee the

moment she arrived. Before stepping through the gate, she turns and waves at three figures, Sissy, Beth, and Joe reunited, waving goodbye with bright smiles. Delphine glances up the steep sandstone bluff and drifts beyond the wooden barricade toward a blossoming orchard. She plucks a plump ruby peach, inhales the sugary fragrance, rolls it over her parched lips, and takes a rapturous bite she'd craved for months. The trees rustle, heavy with peaches falling and collecting in her lifted skirt. Mesmeric laughter and a familiar lullaby pervade the orchard as her image and voice dissolve in a rain of pink blossoms.

DESCENDANTS

PRESENT-DAY MAGNOLIA SUNRISE

SPELLBOUND, SIMONE STEPS FROM THE LONG-DRAINED bathtub, exits the suite, and climbs three flights to the unlocked nursery. She wanders toward the closet to a loose floorboard, pulls out a wooden box, weeping over timeworn books. Dusk fades, weakening Delphine's grip on Simone, who now sleeps against the closet wall. She drifts toward her favorite chair, humming a lullaby. "Rock a bye, my baby bye . . ." The rocker sways, pitching her voice across the room, waning with sunrise.

> *"Rock a bye, my baby bye;*
> *To take a baby gal so fair,*
> *To young missus, waitin' there;*
> *When all was quiet as a mouse,*
> *In ole Massa's big fine house . . ."*

The rocker slows and grows still as her image and voice dissolve with sunrise.

Moments later, Simone breaks through Delphine's last hours with a loud wheeze, waking in a blanket on the closet floor with Parker crouched in a worried stoop beside her. Lost to her whereabouts, she glances around the empty wardrobe, into the room beyond, and lowers her gaze from the bright ceiling light to her bare feet. At once, aware of her nudity beneath the blanket, she draws her knees to her chest and sits upright, abashed. "Wha . . . how . . . where am I? How did I get here?"

Parker raises his hands, palm open to show he's no threat. "Calm down. You're safe. Nothing happened here. You wandered upstairs into the third-floor bedroom adjoining my suite. I found you a few minutes ago."

Simone clutches the blanket to her chest, eyes widening in disbelief. "Oh, God, without clothes? How embarrassing. I've never sleepwalked, ever. No one saw me, I hope."

"Don't worry. The closet was too dark to see anything but your outline. I draped you in the comforter at once."

"Parker, I'm so sorry."

"No apologies needed."

"I assure you I've never done anything like this before." Simone drops her face to her knees, mumbling into the blanket. "The last thing I remember is taking a bath . . ." *And the rolling peach and eerie quiet*. She lifts her head, staring into the room. "What time is it?"

"Six in the morning—"

"Six? It was just night. I was taking a bath. Have I been here the entire evening?"

"Ten minutes at most. Your footsteps woke me." Parker recalls the patter of feet crossing the creaking floor toward the rustling closet door and the faint weeping and singing. He'd risen from his bed and entered the adjacent room as a figure vanished in the swaying chair. He turned, catching Simone's nude body inside the closet, and at once covered her with a blanket. Saving her embarrassment, he'd lied, for he'd seen more than he admitted.

Images of Delphine's life emerge in Simone's mind as though she'd lived every abject moment of her existence, even her painful death. She sits straighter under Parker's gaze. "You must think I'm crazy wandering up here without clothes."

His brows crease with a wry grin. "Nah!" he says with a dismissive wave of the hand. "Guests walk around nude all the time."

Simone titters and lowers her gaze.

"And no, I don't think you're crazy."

She scrunches her face, more uncomfortable with his lie. He's just being polite like her dad with witty un-truths to ease an awkward moment. His behavior sug-gests he'd seen her body, but he's too much of a gentleman to admit it. She rejoins with humor to dispel unease. "I descended a watery hole to wonderland and emerged in the wrong place." Parker's chortle lightens unease for a moment until thoughts of Delphine perturb her again. "I was in the tub and . . ." she says and pauses, afraid she'll appear even crazier.

"What happened in the tub?"

"Nothing," she lies, lifting her gaze from Parker to the slanted ceiling.

The nursery . . . I'm in Delphine's room.

She glances about the space, now a walk-in closet, the place Delphine's curtained Dutch box bed was lo-cated. The area evokes images of Massa Henry pulling the mattress from the creaky wood frame to the floor.

Yellow damask walls with bluebirds and butterflies perched on green vines are a forgotten memory now painted pastel blue over a tufted platform bed. A spot where white lace flowed over a canopy crib to the floor. The striped, white-and-blue rocking horse Delphine bumped into during her escape remains a precious an-tique, invoking a poignant farewell. Simone fixes her gaze on a haunting spot dappled in window light, a place where Delphine read to the twins and longed to return, the bright white rocker once a muted green. Lorelei's raspy voice echoes a ghostly wail from her crimson canopy bed in a Victorian room swathed in green damask harlequin walls and rich Persian rugs now eggshell white with polished wooden floors.

"The nursery was so real."

"It was a nursery years ago."

"Delphine showed me . . ." Simone pivots toward the loose plank in the corner. "The carving's still here," she mumbles, running her finger over imperceptible words faded into the wood.

"So, Delphine's presented herself to you, too?"

"You've seen her?"

Parker nods again. "When I returned to the States several years ago, I woke in the spot where you're sitting just as disturbed, holding that antique writing box," he divulges. "Every time I removed it from the closet, Delphine placed it back under the planks, where she wants it to stay." Parker turns the closet light on and reads, "The twins were born to Delphine Randolph in 1862." "No matter how many times I read this, I still sense her angry, firm grip on the vibrating knife craving into the planks. Amelia and I found the nursery furniture in the attic, and just as she'd showed me in dreams, she'd chiseled those same words into the crib," he explains.

Images of Delphine snaking beneath the high Dutch box bed flash before her as if she'd performed the actions, now a permanent memory. Simone lifts the loose plank and examines the empty hollow. "Are the books inside the box?" she asks, lifting the box at her side.

"Yes, where they've remained since Delphine fled to Union camps."

Three distressed books stacked atop each other lie inside, the top book spotted. "It's wet," she mutters, wary of lifting the fragile books with unraveling bindings.

Parker clears his throat, recalling the weeping moments ago, an event that happens every dawn. "Those are your tears."

"Mine?"

"Well, Delphine's tears manifested through your eyes. She brought you to where most mornings she weeps over those books."

She hadn't removed her makeup last night. Picturing her mascara-smudged face, she wipes under her eyes and over her cheeks. "You sure I was crying?"

"Your eyes are red."

Simone blinks away the blurriness she'd assumed was remnants of sleep. "This happened to you?"

Parker nods. "Amelia found me bewildered with bloodshot eyes in the same spot. For a moment, relief washed over me as though I, not Delphine, had escaped the contraband camp. Delphine knew she'd died, but in death she found freedom, although now she is stuck between two worlds. The place where her bones exist and the home she desired here with the twins."

"The images were so real . . . . Her soul remains with us."

"So we can tell her story and never forget."

Simone lifts one book at a time from the box. Stories she'd read many times as a child. *The Night Before Christmas. The Comic Adventures of Old Mother Hubbard, and her Dog. Grimm's Fairy Tales*. "Delphine learned to read and write from these stories."

"They comforted her when troubled."

She lifts an antique fountain pen from the bottom of the box.

Parker narrows his gaze. "She used the pen to write, but I never found evidence of her script. She must have discarded note pads or whatever she used to write fearing Lorelei's discovery." Parker sits on the floor with a heavy sigh and folds his legs, steepling his fingers at his chin.

Alert to the shift in his body language, Simone

places the books back in the box and grips her knees closer to her chest with raised brows. "Is something wrong?"

He releases a breath, holding Simone's gaze for a quiet moment. No matter how many times he's divulged this story to others, it still gives him pause, apprehensive of their reaction. "Delphine wanted others to recognize she not Lorelei Randolph was the children's mother. It's the reason you're here, Simone."

"What do you mean?"

"When you asked what happened to Delphine at her portrait yesterday, I wasn't ready to divulge such an intricate story, one I'd planned to explain today." He lifts his head toward the wardrobe ceiling and glances around the space with a wry grin. "I couldn't have chosen a better spot to share our history."

"Our history?"

Parker nods. "Soon after I returned from London to assume ownership of Magnolia, on my first night back, Delphine's visitations began, and they didn't stop until I told her story.

"Wait a minute. It just dawned on me we're experiencing the same dreams. Why you and me?"

Parker cups his mouth, blowing air into his hands, and states straightforwardly, "Only her offspring have these dreams. We're Delphine's descendants. Her connection is powerful, even in death." Parker pauses, expecting a reaction, but not a wrinkle creases her face. He perceives the next revelation will rouse a response and heartache. "Your mother was just as silent."

"Mom? Lily?"

Parker nods. "We spoke days before she passed. I'm sorry for your loss, Simone. Lily was interested in knowing more and planned to meet me here at Magnolia. When she explained her daughter worked for *Happy Brides Magazine*, owned by one of my dearest friends, I concluded the universe intervened. Such schemes aren't mere chance. Bridgette and I contrived a pretense to bring you here. I apologize for the deception. There is a story, but not the one you'd planned to write." Parker perceives trouble beneath her stoic expression. He'd hug her, but she might reject his comfort.

"I wondered why Bridgette sent me on another assignment so soon. What if I had refused the job?"

"Then I would have phoned you." His brows knit, wondering if she's always phlegmatic when receiving shocking news?

Noticing Parker's furrowed brows, she shakes her head, patting his hand for reassurance. "I'm not angry just relieved to have answers and my sanity," she says with a quiet chuckle. "Why didn't Mom or Dad tell me?"

"I suspect Lily didn't have time to tell either of you before her death."

"Mom tried to tell me about Delphine in my dreams. She wants me here to know my relation to her." Simone wraps her arms tighter about her legs with a grieved sigh. "Such pain. Delphine lamented till her last breath about abandoning the twins." She gazes toward the area where the crib once stood. The spot where Delphine said farewell to the twins. "What became of the children?"

"Henry Randolph accepted the boys and Delphine's firstborn as his own . . ."

"As he should. They were his babies."

"He accepted his responsibility. Whether out of love or obligation, we will never know. But the children inherited the plantation, and so did their descendants."

"How did you tell her story?"

"Do you recall the hymns rising from the bluff in the dream?"

"How can I forget? It's ingrained forever."

"At the university, I dabbled in poetry a bit but gave it up, saving the world from another bad poet," he says with a titter and headshake. "When I started writing her story, words flowed from my pen in stanzas, the guide I believe Delphine. When the dreams persisted, I knew they'd continue unless I shared the poem. At Natchez Museum of African American History and Culture's front desk, I left the poem with an anonymous letter for the director. Months later, a permanent display on thousands of freed slaves who lost their lives behind contraband camps in the Devil's Punchbowl hung on the museum wall."

Parker?! He's Ella's anonymous poet. "Did the dreams stop?"

"Yes, but Delphine's children's posterity still haunted me. Through genealogy, I uncovered the twins and her firstborn's descendants, which led to you and your mother."

Parker's rapid eye blinks call attention to his thick lashes, which resemble Delphine's, and now she realizes, her mother's. Ah, she thinks. He hugged her when she arrived because she's his long-lost relative. "We're distant cousins?" she asks in a tone more like a statement.

"We're kin through a long bloodline. We might have lived our entire lives unaware if not for Delphine."

"Anyone with a drop of her blood could have these dreams."

"Delphine's descendants might be extensive."

Simone gathers the blanket around her breast, squeezes her thighs together, and pushes herself off the floor. Folding the comforter more tightly around her body, she strolls from the closet toward the rocker glowing in the soft morning light. The spot where Delphine read to the twins and had many times considered leaping through the open window. "She was a prisoner here."

"Every slave was a prisoner, living an awful existence. Though Delphine never toiled the fields, she suffered a shameful ignominy under Lorelei and Henry's roof. This suite will forever belong to Delphine and her descendants. My wife, Amelia, is four months pregnant."

"Congratulations. A boy?"

Parker's brows arch.

"Baby blue," she says, glancing at the wall.

"Ahh, the color. I stripped and painted the walls last month when we decided to restore the room as a nursery and dragged the rocking horse and rocking chair from the attic."

"Is that wise . . . I mean, with Delphine's visitations?"

"She'd never harm her blood, family. Simone, Delphine only wants kin to recognize their heritage and to tell others what happened after she escaped the plantation. For days, she haunted my dreams until I yielded. Unfortunately, Lily's heart wasn't strong enough to handle the dreams. Several of our ancestors died from heart arrhythmias, which I believe Lily also had. I'm surprised doctors hadn't caught it before her death."

"That's what I said to Dad. Arrhythmias?"

"Yes. Genealogical research showed several relatives died from sudden heart attacks. For my own peace of mind, I had my heart examined. Doctors explained familial heart conditions can skip a generation, as it did mine. I believe Delphine's low body fat from starvation, exposure, and giving birth triggered heart failure while she slept. Have you been tested?"

"Yes, Dad and I saw doctors after Mom passed. Test results came back good. No heart issues." Simone recalls Lily clutching her chest in the dream. She was trying to tell her. "I didn't believe Mom died from heart failure. Now I know the truth. The dreams triggered the heart attack."

"Simone, the dreams won't stop until you tell her tragedy. How you communicate the narrative is your choice. With your writing experience, you'll find the proper forum."

Simone slides her hand along the rocker, tilting it back and forth, recalling what she'd learned in school about slavery. "I'd never heard of the Devil's Punchbowl. Why isn't the forced starvation of thousands of freed slaves written in history books?"

"Why aren't the stories of Black Wall Street or Native Americans told? Such atrocities are stains on this country's history. No one wrote about our ancestor's past, unrecorded narratives told by word of mouth for generations. Growing up in Natchez, various versions resonated as more myth than fact. But after Delphine's dreams, the truth is undeniable."

Simone nods in agreement, despite never hearing the term Black Wall Street. But given the context of the conversation, she presumes it's another historical tragedy, one she'll research later, too embarrassed to ask. "I wish others could see what we saw."

"Delphine's bloodline is sizable and still growing. Many more will know the truth."

Simone walks to the window and gazes at the colorful garden where slave cabins once existed. "What happened to Delphine's firstborn, the twins, and Josie?"

Parker rises from the floor toward Simone and stares at the yard. "The twins designed the garden."

"The twins?"

Parker nods. "They demolished the cabins and extended Josie's garden. Amelia and I had a brick walkway paved around the periphery and placed benches alongside the live oaks. We strove to maintain the twin's original design and added a few more annuals and perennials to expand Josie's garden and eradicate an ugly history. The twins planted many herbs over the years: basil, parsley, rosemary, sage, thyme, sorrel, onions, chives, just to name a few. Our chef picks fresh herbs and vegetables for meals just as Josie had for

Lorelei and as she did later when she was the mistress of the house."

"The garden looks like a colorful quilt."

"Hmm, yea, I've never seen it that way, but you're right." Parker throws her a side glance, then gazes at a trail he's observed many evenings. "It might console you to know I've glimpsed Delphine near the garden at night. Whenever she materializes, fireflies assemble near the trees," he says, pointing at the overgrown passage through which she had escaped with Benoit. "She raced from the woods toward a petite woman and young man standing in the garden."

"Josie and Benoit?"

"Yes. I near bawled when a young girl, I believe her firstborn, ran toward Delphine. Then the most miraculous thing happened. Two identical men drifted from the house toward them."

"The twins?"

"Yes. The five gathered in a hug, then Delphine lifted her firstborn in a joyous twirl. A swarm of fireflies bathed them in light right before they vanished. I've seen these flashes only twice, but it's a comfort knowing they've reunited."

Simone's eyes mist over envisioning the six together. "She's reunited with her family and firstborn in death."

"Yes. I believe so."

"Don't her visits frighten you?"

"The first time, but not anymore. I've grown as accustomed to Delphine as I have this creaking home and its persistent cool spots. She's a harmless essence in the woodwork. And to answer your question about their fate, Josie held Delphine's place in the home after her escape. A year later, consumption took Lorelei. Josie wasn't just a cook or mammy to Delphine's children. She was Henry's common-law wife until he died at seventy-five. They raised the children together. Josie passed soon after Henry, leaving Delphine's offspring as Magnolia's lawful heirs."

"The twins never left?"

"Nope. Both married and raised their families under this roof. So did my father, a descendant of the twins. They were astute business owners and ran Magnolia better than the previous proprietors. They have a long-standing store downtown that still carries their name, Jack and Jon's General Store. The twins' names were Jackson and Jonathan."

"What happened to Delphine's grand and great-grandchildren?"

"Many lived in Natchez. Others scattered across the country. Delphine's firstborn, Sylvie, wed a local man. They lived in Natchez many years after starting a family. Later, they settled in Baton Rouge. That's how I traced Lily as Sylvie's descendant."

"Sylvie . . . it's good finally knowing her name."

"Sylvie Randolph, later Hardy when she married Emile Hardy. Simone, you have distant cousins from the twins right here in town. Lily was speechless when I mentioned a specific name. She explained Ella Davis was a lifelong friend."

Simone's eyes widen. "You're kidding? Ella?"

KIN

THREE HOURS LATER, AWASH IN DELPHINE'S ESSENCE AND her newfound heritage, Simone wanders to the computer and opens the document she started the night before, glowering at the blank screen. Every word she'd typed gone. "Impossible . . ." Mystified, she toggles through several files, recalling that she'd clicked save before closing the laptop. After imbibing three heady, king-sized champagne flutes, the screen blurred in her vision. Did she delete the file?

With an immediate realization, she smacks her forehead. "There is no assignment." She snickers and slumps into the chair. Even though it's a bogus assignment, there's a great need to write the article, given her ties to the home's history. But what happened to the document? It didn't simply vanish unless . . .

"Was it you?"

A quiet breeze sweeps through the room, stroking her nape, and straightening Simone's back as she expects a temperature drop and a rolling peach to appear.

"Are you behind me?"

Unafraid, she glances side to side, sniffing around the chair, her pulse beating with compassion, not fear after experiencing Delphine's tragic life. Parker's words come to her again reassuring her Delphine won't harm her own blood. Simone swivels toward the sunny honeymoon suite bright with light from the open windows and patio door. She strolls into the steamy morning toward the garden near the wooded descent. *People will know what happened there.*

"I will write your story," she whispers, standing in the exact spot where Delphine had snatched her wrist. Dream images of the messy peach pulsing in her palm evoke Delphine's difficult delivery. The bite into the bloody peach and Delphine gnawing through the gelatinous umbilical cord are analogous. Simone folds her arms around her waist, recalling her phantom childbirth spasms.

"I wish you'd escaped the camp, found a better life up north, and seen your children alive again." Unmoving, she peers at the shrubbery, imagining Delphine materializing with a reply although she knows she can't and won't. Delphine is omnipresent, forever knowing and watching, she believes. Sighing, she strolls out of the oppressive heat back to the laptop. Three imperative words occupy the screen that was blank moments ago.

"TELL MY STORY."

The supplication mystified her days ago; not anymore. Delphine's not asking but demanding she fulfills an obligation. For two hours, Delphine's world spills onto the page: Her confinement in the nursery as a wet nurse. The psychological and sexual abuses by Lorelei and Henry. The concealed pregnancies Lorelei feigned as her own. The escape to disease-infested contraband camps. The forced starvation of thousands of freed slaves. And Delphine and her newborn's wrongful death in the Union Army camp.

When she types the last word, energy that gripped her mind and hands eases away, leaving her drained and tearful. She wipes her eyes, staring at the screen with immediate relief and an urgent question. How will she publicize the story for others to read? Bridgette . . .

A muffled ringtone breaks her thought. She fetches the cell phone from her handbag with swelling eyes. *Oh no, lunch!*

"Ella, hi."

"Child, I expected you ten minutes ago."

"I'm so sorry. This has been a crazy morning. Ella, I have much to tell you. I'll be there in a flash."

~

Thirty-five minutes later, a modest, pale yellow, two-story cottage appears as Simone veers the car onto a sloping tree-lined driveway. A sense of déjà vu assails her. "Why does the home look so familiar?" She has never been to Ella's home. She reasons it's just a common architecture in Mississippi.

Parking the car, she sits frozen a moment, pondering Ella's reaction to their kinship. *Has Parker told her? Did Mom divulge they're cousins before she passed? No, Ella could never keep their relations a secret, not this long.* Given Parker's poem and the museum exhibit, she's aware of the Devil's Punchbowl. And being Delphine's descendant, she's no doubt experienced the dreams. Lost in mental queries, she's startled by Ella's voice.

"Moni, you gonna just sit there?" Ella asks, tilting her head, sashaying toward the car in a stunning floral maxi dress that halters at her neck. Bright dandelions shimmy with the sway of her petite frame, her body like Josie's—short in stature, slender and wiry.

Why hadn't she noticed the similarities? She and Lily could be sisters. Their stature and mannerisms are the same. The noonday sun strikes her oval eyes, brightening warm cinnamon irises like Delphine's and Lily's as she approaches.

Simone exits the rental straight into her open arms.

"I didn't mean to startle, but you sat stiller than a

statue when I yelled from the porch. Is somethin' wrong?"

"No, no, absorbed in thought."

She releases her embrace and studies Simone's face. "Well, stop your ponderin' and come inside the house." She remains fixed, awestruck. "Lord, I'm lookin' at your mama. The hair is lovely, Moni. Just like Lily." Her eyes narrow in a pensive daze before she clears her throat and motions toward the house.

They stroll past two buzzing bees hovering over a sweet-smelling flower patch, arousing the stinging bite from her childhood. As they draw closer to the porch, an impression strikes her again. "The home looks so familiar, but I don't recall ever visiting."

"Moni, you were too young to remember. You were just three when Lily brought you for Christmas. It was the best holiday with y'all here. You zoomed around the house on that red, three-wheel scooter your dad gave you for Christmas. Drove your momma crazy. When you rode onto the porch and fell off the stairs, Lily hid the scooter. You kicked a fit, bawled yourself to sleep on my sofa."

"Hmpf . . . I recall falling off a scooter, but I thought it happened at home." She rubs the crescent-shaped scar on her elbow, a permanent reminder of the childhood fall.

Shaking her head back and forth, Ella stares at the six porch steps where Simone tumbled. "Goodness gracious, child. Lily was beside herself when she saw you sprawled lifeless on the ground. The fall stunned you into silence for a moment," she explains with a slight chuckle. "When you came around, you wailed so loud it pulled my neighbors from their houses. It's a blessin' you fell sideways and not headfirst."

Simone dissects Ella's face, noticing striking parallels: Cinnamon eyes. Thick lashes. A subtle flare of the nostrils. Round chin. The unmistakable features of Delphine's descendants. "Why didn't you ever visit Baton Rouge?"

Ella's brows and forehead wrinkle over her narrowed eyes. "Moni, I visited many times when you were a child."

"I'm sorry, I don't remember."

"Sometimes, I'd visit for a day or two on the weekends. I even babysat you when Rod and Lily needed alone time. But it became more difficult to visit with my job and tryin' to raise a family. I believe you were in first grade the last time I took care of you."

"First grade . . . Wow, that's a while ago. Hmm, I remember someone babysitting once. But I never had a clear image of the face."

"You were young. I should have visited more often."

"And we should have, too."

In front of Ella's home, Simone notices several cars parked along the narrow street. "Looks like someone's having a gathering."

Ella smiles and grabs her arm. "Let's get out of the heat."

Inside, crowded bookshelves line polished floors, overstuffed armchairs, and gleaming tables. Not a speck of dust is visible. The smell of baked goods wafts from the kitchen, sweet as a bakery. Ella must spend her days cleaning, cooking, and reading, a passion she and Lily share. A variety of African art adorns lemon walls, lemon the dominant color on the main floor. Family photos rest atop of a wooden console behind a tan, pleated couch. A photo of teenage Ella and Lily grabs her attention. The two adolescents with a striking resemblance could be sisters.

Following Simone's gaze, Ella lifts the frame from the console with a wistful sigh. "I love this photo of your mom. We were inseparable in high school. People teased and said we're joined at the hip. And we were." She stares at the picture with a chuckle, her bosom heaving with a fond memory. "No matter how busy our lives, we spoke every day. I miss her phone calls."

"So do I. Ella, there's something I need—"

"I know, child." Ella's chin and brows dip, assuming a guilty expression.

"Know what?"

"We're family."

"Why'd—"

"I didn't tell you because it wasn't the right time with your mom's death." Ella takes Simone's hand, seating her on the couch. "Growin' up, I felt a strong, inexplicable connection to Lily, a bond resolved the day Parker contacted us. Lily called me the night she'd discovered our ties to the Randolph family. I was more than shocked to learn my best friend was kin. We planned to meet Parker at Magnolia Sunrise, but . . . the Lord had other designs. I urged Parker to wait until you and Roderick had time to mourn Lily's death and after your trip to France. That's when Parker informed me of his plan. Well, you know the rest."

"I knew you withheld information yesterday."

"Lyin' is never easy. I almost broke my promise to Parker. He'd asked me to wait until you two met and you saw Magnolia Sunrise."

Quiet chatter resounds from the rear of the home.

"You have guests?"

"People who've been waitin' to meet you."

"People?"

"Your kin. A few of Delphine's local descendants. Come on, lunch is out back," she says, grabbing her hand and leading her to the enclosed porch.

Around the colorful table, replete with southern food and spirits, sit several generations of Delphine's descendants, ranging from adolescents to senior citizens. Skin tones vary from the darkest of dark to the lightest of light.

The veranda lights with smiles and gleeful hand

waves as chairs screech back from the table. "Welcome, cousin!" they greet in unison, approaching and stating their names with firm embraces.

In Simone's astonishment, fifteen names sound in one continuous stream, forgotten, unrepeatable. The overwhelming acceptance into an unexpected family causes tears to well up in her eyes. Lost for words, she smiles and wipes a tear, wishing Delphine could see her wonderful progeny. "Hello, family."

ANTIQUITY RISES AGAIN

SIMONE WRINGS HER HANDS, STARES AT THE PACKED Samsonite, wrestling with staying a few days longer, though she's been in Natchez seven days longer than she'd planned. She relinquished the Bluff Side suite to honeymooners for the nursery, per Parker when her reservation ended a week ago. He's been a gracious host, but since his wife, Amelia, returned a day ago, her being only a wall away and sharing a bath is intrusive. For the first time tonight, their low, intimate voices and amorous laughter resound from the master suite, causing uneasiness. She grimaces, imagining her proximity makes them just as uncomfortable. *No. It's inconsiderate to stay longer, back to Brooklyn in the morning.* With a resolute sigh, she closes the luggage and pulls it toward the foot of the bed.

Light fades in the far corner, pulling her gaze toward the dark laptop screen, dimmed in power save. She ambles over and touches the pad. Delphine's story emerges again, an article completed a day ago after gathering information from her descendants, people who've lived in the same town, unaware of their relations until Parker. Now a cohesive group, they're committed to a common cause, telling a factual account never told, one they won't let others forget—the tragic deaths of thousands of freed slaves in Natchez contraband camps. Historical narratives future generations will retell.

After learning of her kin, Simone was eager to tell her father what transpired and phoned him after Ella's luncheon. Everything flew from her mouth before Roderick could say a word. The next morning, he arrived unannounced at Ella's with an overnight bag and Lily's Bible. Just as Mom conveyed in dreams, Parker's poem, transcribed on Ella's oatmeal stationery, lay tucked between the pages of Matthew 7:18.

"A healthy tree cannot bear bad fruit, nor can a diseased tree bear good fruit."

The verse evoked images of Lily covered head to toe in blossoms, a dream she tried to interpret, the meaning obvious after everything she'd experienced. Ella said the verse is a parable of false prophets. Dad believes Lily picked a random spot in the Bible without forethought. Neither Ella nor Dad dreamt of Lily. Simone pressed her point and described the backward words in the dream, deciphered the day after she woke in the nursery. Written in reverse, Lily's words, "Senob deirub woleb s'zehctan sffulb," means "Bones buried below Natchez's bluffs." Lily wanted her to know where Delphine was buried.

After further analysis of the branches blossoming around Lily and the dark limbs spiraling up her arm from Delphine's poisonous nails, Simone surmised a deeper meaning. Lily used the verse as an allegory of Delphine and her descendants.

"Don't you understand," she'd implored Dad and Ella, "Delphine is the healthy tree, the 'good fruit' her children and descendants. The diseased tree is slavery and the Devil's Punchbowl, a tainted harvest of 'bad fruit'—death, hatred, and systemic racism."

Following her persuasive tirade, they soon understood and supported her analysis. Lily chose the verse, realizing she'd grasp the meaning even without her intervention. For two days, she and Dad stayed at Ella's home recounting special times with Mom and her childhood with Ella, things they never knew. Dad's lingering doubt was put to rest after learning Lily's heart condition runs in the family. When he mentioned Lily's ashes, Ella was less than thrilled to hear the urn sit on the mantelpiece. She must have searched her memory the entire night.

As Dad prepared to leave the following morning, Ella described a perfect spot for Lily's cremains in Natchez National Historic Park. A magnificent waterfall cascading into a flowing creek. "Lily always loved that spot. It gave her much comfort," Ella explained. Once or twice, Lily mentioned a waterfall, but Simone never knew its location. She and Dad agreed unanimously to return to Natchez next month for a small memorial and to release Lily's ashes into the waterfall.

Simone pulls her attention back to the laptop and Delphine's story. The article will appear in *Vocal*, an online nonprofit magazine she'd considered working for before *Happy Brides*. An organization that uncovers and reports untold events in American history. She couldn't resist writing an article on Magnolia Sunrise's honeymoon specials, which Bridgette will feature in *Happy Brides'* July edition.

She glimpses the time before closing the laptop. It's late, she thinks, peering out the window at dusk muting the colorful garden, hoping to catch Delphine's ghostly family reunion. For a week, she'd watched and waited, only to fall asleep and wake to Delphine's dissolving image in the rocker. Tonight, she's determined to stay awake with a brisk walk in the garden.

Simone wanders from the house to the garden's brick path and on toward a bench facing what was once

Slave Row. For twenty minutes, with crickets and other critters serenading her, she imagines the plantation centuries ago with miles of cotton and tobacco fields, overworked slaves in one-room cabins slumbering before another toilsome day arrives.

Gnats and other insects hover and buzz in her ear. She swats the muggy air, swiveling her head to a single firefly. Then a charge rustles the atmosphere. The hem of her gauzy pants flutter at her ankles. A sweet scent rides the breeze. Tiny lights dot the night, multiplying through a thicket of trees. Simone sits straight, expectant, holding her breath, gasping at the advancing specter. Delphine emerges from the shrubbery, pregnant and aglow in clean slave clothes, not the dusty, tattered dress of her dream. She drifts through flowers that weren't there during her time. Spectral laughter fills the garden as a woman and man materialize. Delphine's faint voice calls, "Maw, Ben . . ."

Every hair vibrates on Simone's skin as she steps from the bench across the path through the pungent herbal garden. Two attractive men materialize, strolling with Simone toward the gathering. She halts and gasps when a night-gowned girl rushes through her body.

Sylvie! Her great-grandmother, five times removed.

Simone reaches out to grab the ethereal child. Sylvie escapes her encircled arms toward the huddled family, caught in Delphine's grasp, twirled in circles with gleeful laughter. Bright fireflies swarm, tunnel, and encompass their vanishing figures, releasing a powerful surge.

Simone's loose blouse flutters as the surge passes through her with Delphine's overwhelming joy. In the center of the garden where they vanished, a tiny light moves forward, splitting into several lights flickering toward her extended hand.

Six fireflies illuminate her arm, merging with her flesh. Simone warms and tingles as though a bright light explodes within, radiating through every cell of her body, flooding her heart with joy and laughter. She drops to her knees, radiant with Delphine's powerful love for her family.

They're together, again.

NOT AGAIN

BATON ROUGE METROPOLITAN AIRPORT

SIMONE FASTENS HER SEATBELT AND QUICKLY TYPES A TEXT she'd meant to send before boarding the airplane, before Bridgette's phone call obliterated the thought:

Parker, you've opened my eyes and heart with a purpose I've searched for for years. Thanks for the inspiration and gift. I'm honored to be a member of your family. I'll see you in a month, cousin.

Simone rereads the text, presses send, and shuts off the mobile as the plane taxis onto the runway. When she closes her eyes, six fireflies glitter in her mind. Six . . . Delphine, Josie, Benoit, Jackson, Jonathan, and Sylvie, she affirms mentally. The gripping, miraculous spectral reunion kept her wired and awake till dawn. She left the garden, sat in the parlor, recounted events of the past weeks, and reaffirmed the earlier decision to freelance at *Vocal* magazine.

As she was curled in a plump parlor armchair, Parker's silent entry startled her from deep thought. He emerged with a glossy book, apologizing for the fright. Simone sat upright, eyes locked on the shiny hardcover design of a healthy blossoming peach tree beneath Magnolia Sunrise, splitting open the four-story Victorian floorboards. Offshoots bursts through the rooftop, launching shingles airborne and crashing to the ground. Many branches sprout twigs that extend and connect to larger limbs. Branches and branches of the Randolph family growing off the binding.

"What an amazing cover."

"This is for you. The Randolph family tree I gift to descendants," Parker had explained, placing the book in her hand and walking toward the dry bar. "Would you care for a glass of bourbon?"

The amber liquid evoked indulgent glasses of malbec she'd inhaled at the farewell-rooftop party in Marseille and the ensuing morning-after-splitting headache she endured racing to catch a flight. "I shouldn't."

"Just a glass. It's your last night at Magnolia Sunrise. Let's toast to family and new beginnings."

She'd considered the short shot glass he held and conceded. "All right. A sip or two can't hurt."

They'd toast to family and new beginnings, down the whiskey in one gulp, and thumbed through many pages of relatives in the glossy book before he joined his wife upstairs, an hour later. As he bent over to hug her goodnight, she welcomed his embrace with a tighter squeeze than the first time they'd met in the yard. She remained in the comfy lounge chair long after Parker returned upstairs. The breadth of descendants he'd located kept her glued to the family tree until the first blush of morning peeped through the windows.

Groggy-eyed, daybreak yanked her from her heritage, upstairs to shower and dress for her early morning flight back to New York. She'd paused as she gathered her bags to leave for the airport, gazed at the blue walls, sloped ceiling, walk-in closet, and garden view beyond the window. Then a familiar, sweet scent gripped her as she walked toward the door and turned the knob. A fleeting question assailed her mind. *Why es-*

cape the nursery, a prison, and return after death? Did she find eternal happiness reunited with her babies?

The rocking chair wobbled with that thought.

She released the doorknob, realizing the momentary impression was Delphine's.

Straightaway the rocker had stilled.

Her gaze affixed to the cream seat-back cushion where she imagined Delphine sat.

The chair tilted back and forth once, an affirmative nod to her mental query.

She'd blinked and responded, "I understand," as though Delphine expected her to do so.

Before she closed the door, she'd smiled and inhaled the evanescent sweetness. Sadness always strikes at the end of assignments and with farewells to new friends. But leaving Magnolia Sunrise, where her ancestry began, is bittersweet poignancy. However, Delphine exists inside her forever. She's her blood—her past, present, and future. As she closed the door, it squeaked, and the lock clicked, evoking Delphine's heartrending escape. She glanced at Parker's bedroom door, then back at the nursery, and had imagined his unborn baby boy's resounding whimpers throughout the corridor. *Delphine will watch over the little one.* Simone released the doorknob and hurried along the passageway, as Delphine had years ago.

The airplane tilts sideways, pulling her attention back to the cramped plane cabin. The Mississippi River comes into view, snaking toward the coast. Two weeks ago, she'd searched along the riverbank for the infamous bowl-shaped gulch. Now, no longer interested in seeing the place many lost their lives, she swiftly pulls the shutter over the window. She was troubled when she arrived, but now she leaves with answers, a new purpose, and an ever-growing family. When the airplane levels, Simone reclines back in the seat, eyes closed, eager to nap.

Ten minutes asleep, she's thrust into a fiery dream, inside a burning building, beneath smoking rubble. An airplane drone overhead. A whistle plummets from the sky, growing closer, shriller, cratering the ground with a rattling explosion nearby. Men and women scream. Children cry. Gunfire pops. Bullets whizz. Chaos grows around her. A blazing man and woman emerge through dense smoke, their frightful, painful roar vibrating the scorching air. Their eyes light on her, mouth agape.

"TELL OUR STORY!"

Their searing hands seize her shoulder, setting Simone aflame.

She screams, jolts upright, swatting phantom flames from her body, startling passengers and the flight attendant racing along the aisle toward her.

No, please, not again!

The End?

History books never mentioned me or my people. Yes, I've seen your world from which we came, that shaped our world, your world, and your children's world, and will shape the world of their children to come. See my story; tell my story so that one day others will know and never forget it.

TAINTED HARVEST

Below the bluffs of Natchez Trace,
The Devil's Eden lies in waste.
A tainted harvest, sinfully laced,
Corse sowed and reaped,
Reptilian chawed, rotted silt loam,
A charnel house,
Below the bluffs of Natchez Trace.
Forsaken souls rise at harvest,
Imparting offerings of history's horrors,
Oh, what bittersweet hymns of sorrow,
Below the bluffs of Natchez Trace.
Beware the crag on summer eves,
She arrives, aggrieved,
Arms replete with plummy treasures.
Oh, how tempting, succulent, sweet,
Yet, wicked to the pitted marrow.
One bite, she'll reveal
A grim genesis of horrors,
Skeletal antiquity,
Deeply seeded,
Root-to-leaf fodder,
For the Devil's harvest,
Below the bluffs of Natchez Trace.
When Sumter thundered, plantations shuttered,

Relented barbarous tricentennial bondage,
Jubilant cries of freedom followed,
'til Union Armies hollered, halt,
Thwarting thousand's glory walk.
Detained, rerouted, entrapped, encamped on
    banks,
Flesh and bone buried where they sank.
Oh, what spoilage stains the bowl-shaped gulch,
Below the bluffs of Natchez Trace.
A forsaken, veritable unwritten history,
A parable of tainted harvest,
Forbidden fruit,
Tacit townsfolk dare not savor,
Oh, what mystery,
Deep in the Devil's Eden,
Below the bluffs of Natchez Trace.

ACKNOWLEDGMENTS

First and foremost, I'd like to thank my family for their immeasurable love and encouragement.

Also, special thanks to my dear friend and fellow author, Lawrence E. Crockett, for suggesting and urging me to write this story. Like many, I knew nothing of the Devil's Punchbowl until a conversation with him a year ago.

Thanks to Next Chapter Publishing, my Editor, Shire Brown, and Cover Designer, Matt Davies for their fantastic work.

Also, I'd like to thank my friends for their constant support and readers for reading my stories.

ABOUT THE AUTHOR

For as long as I can remember, I've had a book in my hand. At the age of seven, I'd often read to my mother at night around the fireplace. A fond memory I'll forever cherish. My origin is Monroeville, Alabama, but at nine-years-old, I moved to New York City—a stark contrast to my natal roots. The Deep South remains firmly ingrained in my soul as I craft worlds from my city dwelling. Often, I've evoked memories of a carefree girl who climbed trees, ran barefoot on Alabama red soil, lolled on green pastures, and traipsed along wooded paths picking blackberries. When I came to live in New York City with my aunt, an actress and educator, I traded tomboy ways for an artistic existence.

I live and work on the Upper East Side of Manhattan where I share my life with family and good friends. But every so often, a familiar aura of sultry breezes, dusk, pitch-black, and haunting Alabama spirits, unseen in the cloak of night, whisper their stories, a place that calls to me when I write. Hopefully, one day I'll capture those experiences on paper.

~

To learn more about E. Denise Billups and discover more Next Chapter authors, visit our website at www.nextchapter.pub.

Tainted Harvest
ISBN: 978-4-86750-783-4
Mass Market

Published by
Next Chapter
1-60-20 Minami-Otsuka
170-0005 Toshima-Ku, Tokyo
+818035793528

10th June 2021